Particular Place and People

Linda Fine Hunt

Trenton, Georgia

Copyright © 2023 Linda Fine Hunt

Print ISBN: 978-1-958889-97-8
Ebook ISBN: 979-8-88531-515-9

All rights reserved. No part of this publication may be reproduced, stored in a retrieval system, or transmitted in any form or by any means, electronic, mechanical, recording or otherwise, without the prior written permission of the author.

Published by BookLocker.com, Inc., Trenton, Georgia.

Printed on acid-free paper.

The characters and events in this book are fictitious. Any similarity to real persons, living or dead, is coincidental and not intended by the author.

BookLocker.com, Inc.
2023

First Edition

Library of Congress Cataloguing in Publication Data
Hunt, Linda Fine
Particular Place and People by Linda Fine Hunt
Library of Congress Control Number: 2023908884

I dedicate this book to the memory of my grandmother, Hilda Kramer Fine (Bubbe). Her courageous life and love shaped who I became. And to David, who gave me everything.

Contents

Prologue: Do Not Skip 1
Chapter 1: 1954 First Lesson 9
Chapter 2: How We Got Here 17
Chapter 3: Eye, News, Costume, Indian 20
Chapter 4: More about the Brodskys...26
Chapter 5: Are There Rules? 34
Chapter 6: Reality of First Grade 37
Chapter 7: Blackie, My Mansion, and a New Book...................43
Chapter 8: I Went Too Far 48
Chapter 9: With My Mom...52
Chapter 10: Mrs. Frank's Vanity Dresser 60
Chapter 11: Work, Create, Build Gifts from Bubbe 67
Chapter 12: Gentile Side of the Neighborhood..........................77
Chapter 13: A Day at the Library 84
Chapter 14: Shortcut..97
Chapter 15: Becoming More of Me 102
Chapter 16: Hanley Junior High School, A Transition 108
Chapter 17: 1966 Diaspora..120
Epilogue 133
Acknowledgments...137
Rendering of 1900 Mansion..139

Prologue: Do Not Skip

For over 200 years, people from various cultures lived at 1433 Partridge Avenue in a limestone mansion built around 1850. In 1954, the surrounding orchards and fields became my home, my friends' homes, and where my grade school stood. The mansion was a place central to my childhood. I still dream and think about it even though it is long gone. The story I am about to tell you has a backstory. Here it is.

I was fortunate to have spoken with Isabella Roberts. She is the granddaughter of John C. Roberts and the daughter of Elzey Meacham Roberts, both prominent men in St. Louis business and society. Isabella was born in 1934. She started our conversation by telling me she was the fifth Isabella on her mother's side of the family. Not liking the name Isabella, she named her daughter Anne. She explained her family first lived at 6330 McPherson Avenue in the Parkview neighborhood of University City near Washington University. Her immediate family consisted of her dad, Elzey Meacham Roberts; her mom, Isabella Wells Roberts; and her brother, Elzey Meacham Roberts, Jr.

"Please call me Bobby. My parents swopped homes in 1944 with my grandmother, Anna Roberts, the widow of John C. Roberts. My grandmother believed the homestead was now too big for her after her husband died." Bobby loved telling the story of her grandmother's dog, Brucy. "After grandmother moved from the homestead on Partridge Avenue to McPherson Avenue, Brucy, a collie, ran away from the McPherson home and showed up at the Partridge Avenue home, three miles away. He loved the homestead. We decided to keep Brucy at the homestead with us. Anna Roberts died in 1954."

I interrupted her, "That is the year we moved into our house on Hazelwood Lane."

Bobby continued, "My grandmother was not warm and fuzzy. She intimidated my mother. My mother always called her Mrs. Roberts. Of course, I never met my grandfather, John C. Roberts. He died nine years before I was born. I do remember the land. It had a little of everything. There was pasture for corn and wheat. On the pasture stood an old empty frame house. My parents told me to stay out of it."

"Just like my mom told me not to visit your homestead." We both broke some rules and became more independent from doing so. "That pasture became my elementary school. What was it like living on this property?"

"My childhood was lonely. There were no playmates in the neighborhood. I attended school at Mary Institute, which was a long drive away. I took a bus home. I learned how to care for the chickens and had a pet goat. We owned horses. My horse was a retired polo pony named Sonja. One day I rode Sonja bareback in the field. The pony took off fast up to a fence, stopped, and threw me on the fence. With injuries, I got up and climbed back on Sonja." I could tell Bobby knew nothing about Elmira Benoist's deadly pony accident just a block away almost 100 years ago.

Bobby spoke modestly at first about her family. She did not think her family was prominent in St. Louis affairs. "That is all you know. You take it for granted."

I explained, "When John C. Roberts died, visitation was on the first floor of the homestead. The newspaper wrote people filled the whole first floor with flowers. People from all walks of life came to pay tribute. They included people who worked in his factories, sold his shoes, printed his newspapers, newsboys, writers, reporters, politicians, judges, lawyers, business owners, and dignitaries from around the country." I quoted the newspaper to Bobby. "It was a tribute from a city, a state, and a nation. It was marked with simplicity in keeping with the life of the man."

"I did not know," she replied. "When I was young, it was during World War II. He had been dead for a long time."

Since she did not care for Anna Roberts, Bobby may not have wanted to know much about her grandfather, John C. Roberts. She preferred to talk about her other grandfather. "My grandfather, Rolla Wells, was mayor of St. Louis during the World's Fair, 1904. He was handsome. I participated in the Veiled Prophet celebrations as a debutant."

Bobby's parents had hired help to manage the homestead. There was a chauffeur. The carriage house where the chauffeur lived remains the last standing building of the homestead, now designated as a historical property. I keep contemplating that if the mansion was not sold in 1963 to the developer, it too would still be standing and designated as a historical property.

Bobby continued, "The cook and housekeeper lived on the third floor. My parents told me not to go up there. It was private quarters. The groundskeeper taught me how to milk a cow. He always wore a white coat when working. He had his own house near the homestead off a gravel road."

"Children were not invited to dinner parties at the home. I remember listening to one such party where my father asked the chauffeur to bring in one of the just-born piglets to show the guests. I could hear the piglet squeal from my room upstairs. I remember exploring the attic and finding an old German helmet from World War I."

I informed her, "Your father, Elzey Roberts Sr., and uncle, John C. Roberts Jr. served in World War I."

"You know a lot about my family."

"It's all in old newspapers."

"My father also owned the radio station KXOK."

"I grew up listening to KXOK in the car and my bedroom. It was my favorite radio station," I told her.

We reminisced about the blue morning glories blooming behind the house. We agreed morning glories were our favorite flowers. She asked if I remembered the rose garden. "No, but I read about the rose garden in newspapers." We chuckled. She was surprised someone would write about the rose garden in the newspaper. "The reporter connected the garden to a social event at your home." I was careful not to call it a mansion. Earlier, she corrected me by saying it was not a mansion. It was her home. She called it a homestead.

I explained how I climbed the beautiful wood staircase to the kitchen when the Seventh-Day Adventist Church owned the home. "I liked visiting the cook. I remember how big the kitchen was." We both remembered it being painted green. There were green tiles. "It looked like the kitchen in the *Downton Abbey* television series." She agreed. "However, I never went any higher than the second floor. I wish I had."

Bobby provided more details, "There was a piano in a music room, and we had a formal dining room. I liked the circular sunroom on the main floor. I remember coal deliveries. Coal had to be shoveled into the furnace every day. The thick stone walls kept the house cool even in the hot St. Louis summers." We paused talking. I wanted her to think of more stories.

"My mother delivered food to the surrounding neighbors during World War II. She delivered food raised on the homestead. She was issued more gasoline coupons for these deliveries. The government rationed gasoline during the War."

For high school, Bobby went to boarding school. She had a celebratory social gathering at the homestead during her sophomore year at Washington University. Bobby was formally introduced to society at this event as a young debutante. Other Veiled Profit debutantes attended. The newspaper (Sept 10 1952 *Post-Dispatch*) reports she came from a line of Veiled Profit Queens. She graduated from Washington University with a degree in art history.

Bobby further explained her mother did a lot of charity work for the Home of the Friendless, an older person's home. After college, Bobby became a caseworker though it was against her parents' wishes. They wanted her to marry instead. I told her I worked as a caseworker when I graduated college. A year later, she moved to Chicago to work as a social worker for the American Red Cross. Her independence was seen throughout her life and gave her a good life. Bobby's life verified setting goals and having free will may be the path to happiness.

She talked about the new home her parents bought. "My parents' new home was very modern. It was in Ladue on the grounds of the St. Louis County Club. I remember the new home's bedrooms had many windows on three sides of each room. My parents hosted my engagement party at the homestead and the wedding reception at the new house."

Her father died eight years after they moved into this new home at the same age her grandfather, John C. Roberts, died. Both were 70.

I found an advertisement published in the *St. Louis Globe-Democrat* Sunday, May 13, 1900. See end of book. It shows a drawing of a home on Partridge Avenue with some features identical to the Roberts' homestead. It says the choice suburban home is stone and sits on six acres with fruits and flowers between Page Boulevard and Olive Road. It has 14 large rooms. Even the sidewalk matches the one I remember. Through email, I asked Bobby to verify that this was a picture of her home. "Yes, it was my place." After John C. Roberts purchased the home in 1905, he bought 27 additional acres of fields and orchards. We ended our conversation with Bobby telling me another story about a path to the fields where my home and school were now.

"On this path bordering both sides were pear trees." I could feel myself getting excited. Bobby was talking about pear trees. Now, another connection was developing. John C. Roberts' path of pear trees led to my backyard. The last remaining pear tree was the one in my backyard. My thoughts went back to me at age three.

I told Bobby, "I treasured that remaining pear tree. It helped me find my house as a child." I told her the story I am about to tell you. I thanked Bobby for telling me about the rows of pear trees. I learned my pear tree was part of a planted pear tree path leading to the homestead from the fields and orchards. When

Particular Place and People

Bobby and her family left 1433 Partridge Avenue in 1953, construction of University Forest Estates began. In 1954, my family moved to this particular place. Bobby's place became my place, and the story begins.

Chapter 1:
1954 First Lesson

There is so much I want to tell. The story begins in 1954 when I was three years old and moved with my parents from an apartment on Kingsbury Boulevard in St. Louis City to a suburb called University City. We moved to a new development, a subdivision, and a new grade school, the third ward within the district in University City. The subdivision was called University Forest Estates. The ad in the newspaper used the word *estates*. Now, I think of estates as big houses on acres of land, just like the original mansion on this property. The hook of using the word estates was that these home buyers who became my neighbors lived in city apartments. Some lived with extended family members. Buying a house in this new subdivision was a chance to own property. A few of my new neighbors were immigrants who had to leave family and all their possessions in Europe to flee the Nazis. Some were newly married, and this was their first residence as a couple. To post-war Americans, the small houses and yards were estates. The homes were 1,200 square feet, and the lots were 5,001 square feet. Rather than a street, I remember it being called a block. "What block do you live on?" a schoolmate might ask.

"Hazelwood Lane," I replied. The other blocks were Willow Tree Lane, White Oaks Lane, and Faris Lane. I know. Why Faris Lane? There is no Faris tree. It was an existing street named after the Faris family. Located on Faris Lane was a bright white stone mansion on a hill. It was behind my mansion. I will talk about my mansion later. At one time, the owners of these two mansions were related, the Faris family and the Benoist family. They wanted to live near each other in country homes. I love history.

Meet my family. Our last name is Fine. That is important because we know who is Jewish by a person's last name. We take pride in our last name. Fine is such a cool name. There is even a song called "She's So Fine." Later in 1964, the Temptations recorded a song called "The Girl's Alright with Me." In it was the line, "She's so fine".

My dad is Hyman Fine. Everyone calls him Hy Fi, short for the High-Fidelity record player. He returned from World War II in 1945. When my parents bought this new house, Dad was about 44 years old. I say "about" because he did not know his birthday. It was in October, going by the Jewish calendar. The year may have been in question, too. For his birthday in America, he picked the middle of the month, October 15th.

I always liked Dad's stories. He smokes pipes and has a beautiful pipe collection. Outside of the house, on our porch, he smoked cigars. He was happy. About 37 years ago, he lived in a Lithuanian village where people tried to kill his family. His immediate family safely traveled to St. Louis. He learned English, graduated grade school, got a good paying job, married a beautiful woman, had two children, drove a Buick, and could sit in the evenings on a porch connected to a lovely house reading the newspaper and smoking his pipe or cigar. Dad was a beautiful whistler with blonde hair and powder-blue eyes.

Mom is more complicated. Her name is Bess. She grew up in St. Louis City, very poor. Her mother, Bertha, spent time gambling on the little money Grandpa Louis earned from painting houses and carpentry work. Grandma's addiction was horse races.

Grandpa's addiction was alcohol. Mom graduated from Soldan High School top of her class. She is a beauty with green eyes. Mom is big-breasted. Boys ask me if I was adopted. She was 35 years old when we moved to this new house. Mom came from a mean mom (I could tell stories) and thought the only way to escape was to marry.

During the war, Mom learned she could be self-sufficient. She explained, "I did not want to be married when your father came home from the war. I stayed. We had you and Gary. We lost our first child. I believed this house was a new beginning." I learned women might compromise their goals for a home, material gain, family, and guilt.

Mom loved to decorate and decorate she did. Dad agreed to all her ideas. Mom designed everything to be forever. The 100% wool carpet in the living room, the custom-made silk draperies, and a wall covered in grass cloth made our place beautiful. We had famous designer furniture now sought out by collectors.

Mom decided to have our house painted redwood. The green roof with redwood gave it a Western and modern feel. Most other houses were white. Mom hated conformity. I was proud of her. She was intelligent, fun, and she could sing. Most of the time, I preferred being with Mom instead of kids my age. We had interesting conversations. It might seem strange she chatted with me as if I was an adult, but that is how Mom and I conversed. My movie star Mom had beautiful red hair and never went outside without wearing lipstick, a tradition I carry on. I loved going through her scarves, makeup, and jewelry drawers.

My brother, Gary, is three years older than me. Picture him with dark brown hair and green eyes. He was the most beautiful baby. I knew this from his baby pictures. We fought a lot. Yet he was my protector. He was rarely home. He had lots of friends.

He read comic books. He took mechanical gadgets apart and sometimes had trouble putting them back together. "He's going to be an engineer," Mom told everyone. If he misbehaved, my parents ordered him to his room. When this happened, he jumped out of his bedroom window and walked down the street to a friend's house. I thought my brother should work for the FBI.

Gary was not into sports much except for ping-pong. He was a champion player. Our parents bought him a weight set. I started lifting these weights because I was so tiny. Gary could play the trumpet, and we attended numerous concerts at our brand-new school, University Forest Elementary School. Gary excelled in math. Why didn't he help me with my math homework? He did teach me how to tie my shoes.

Gary made the best French fries because he left the potato skins on. It was a dangerous activity for kids at home, alone. I had crushes on some of his friends. Terry was my favorite. We played hide-and-go-seek at night. We ran around with lightning bugs or fireflies till our parents called us in. Our neighborhood was safe.

Me? I just turned sixteen. I decided to write about a particular place and people. In other words, I am writing about culture. Different environments fascinate me. Environments may determine who we become. Lucky for me, I grew up in University City, Missouri. This place supported my religion, education, and my dreams.

People describe me as impatient. She is "always on to the next activity." I tell them I was born six weeks too soon and weighed three and a half pounds. I met the world early and tiny. I had a lot to accomplish. For example, I wanted to write like Louisa May Alcott.

I am not a typical girl. Sure, I loved to dress up and look pretty. However, I prefer to wear boys' clothes. I raided Gary's closet for shirts and sweaters. I have long wavy blonde hair. My eye color is unique. It is called hazel, teal with gold. It is a rare color. I am too skinny. I will explain why later.

When I was younger, I collected books, dolls, coins, stamps, butterflies, rocks, and shells. I had crushes on a few boys. What was atypical was my independence at an early age. I questioned the rules. I told adults what I thought of them if I did not respect them. I defended myself. If I couldn't, I brought Mom into the battle. As I said, Mom and I spent a lot of time together. Mom should have told people, "My daughter is going to be a writer." She never did. She advised me I was going to be a secretary for a lawyer. "Then you will marry the lawyer."

We only had one car at first. Dad bought expensive Buicks. We even had a pink Buick at one time with fins. Our new house was close to everything. The grocery store was just a mile away. Mom and I walked to National Food Store, or we could walk a quarter of a mile to Page Boulevard and catch a bus to anywhere. My school was just a block away, on Partridge Avenue. The swimming pool at Heman Park was a mile walk. We walked to Pennsylvania Food Shop and bought penny candy. It was paradise. We had everything we needed. Later, Dad became instrumental in developing a Jewish War Veterans building on the corner of Partridge Avenue and Olive Street Road. I lived in a Jewish community. I knew nothing else.

The area was called University Forest. Yet, there were few trees. I later learned my subdivision was built on an orchard of various fruit trees. Giant oak trees and woods were just on the south side of my grade school. To the north, large trees surrounded my mansion. I call it "my mansion" because it was everything to me.

I preferred interesting places and adults. My first visit to my mansion was a little scary. I did not understand time, and I thought I might see dinosaurs. Mom explained dinosaurs lived long ago, and they were all dead. That made me feel safe walking over to my mansion. On the mansion grounds was an arbor bigger than my house. There was a playground with the best swings, beautiful gardens, and magical woods. The concrete reflecting pond was dry and in bad shape. Best of all was the limestone gazebo. Seeing the gazebo for the first time, I learned the word, charming. My mansion might have been 100 years old. Exploring my mansion and the grounds taught me the word, magnificent. I fell in love with this place.

Our subdivision was taking shape. The city planted oak trees along the streets. Our house stood out because it had a large pear tree in the corner of the backyard that bore fruit. Mom baked me a pear fruit pie once.

At first, all the houses sat in dirt; mud when it rained. No fences existed. It was my "oyster" (my mom quoting Shakespeare) where I learned the freedom of exploration and drove my desire to experience the world. At age three, I began walking through the neighbors' backyards from my backyard. As I continued to walk through the backyards, the ground got muddy. Mud is typical at construction sites. I only made it to the second backyard west of my house. What stopped me? I could no longer walk. I sank into the mud. I was stuck. I could not move. I was lucky I had not seen Westerns, the movies where men died sinking in quicksand. I was not afraid. I had choices. Crying would only get me a runny nose with tears down my face. Doing nothing left me at the mercy of someone accidentally finding me. Screaming my head off could get me the help I needed. I yelled for help. I learned action works. I made the right choice. Lucky for me, no one had air conditioning, though the builder mentioned air conditioning in the list of options.

Windows were open. Mrs. Farb heard me scream and came to my rescue. She lifted me out of the mud. We walked to the front of her house onto Hazelwood Lane. But I could not identify my home. We walked past the Garman's home, between the Farb's house and mine. Then I saw the pear tree behind our house. I recognized my home only by the location of the pear tree in the backyard. "That's my house." We walked to the back door through the screened porch. Mrs. Farb delivered me to my mom, covered in mud.

Upon seeing me, Mom exclaimed, "Thank God you are okay!" There was no mention of the ruined shoes. Mom was not stressed back then. Probably, I walked out of the house, unknown to her. That is what explorers do.

A few years after my first adventure, lightning struck the pear tree. The tree's trunk was black from the fire. It fell, and my parents removed it. I missed the pear tree. It was the first tree I loved. I argued that I wanted the branches to remain in our yard so I could climb on them. I lost. I now wish I saved a branch as a decoration for my bedroom.

Years later, I talked to Mrs. Farb's daughter, Susan, about this story. Susan related the story to her mom. "Yes, it did happen," Susan reported back to me. Mrs. Farb remembered rescuing me. "Please tell your mom thank you from me. Not only did she rescue me, but she also remembered my first memory."

I learned before exploring to make sure someone knows where I am going and report my return. Most importantly, I will thank those who helped me, even if it is years later.

Chapter 2:
How We Got Here

Mom explained, "Dad and I were looking at new houses on Vernon Avenue in University City. The houses were tiny, nothing special, but we had outgrown our apartment on Kingsbury Boulevard. The developer, Sam Ladd, told us to visit his newest University City development. He called it a subdivision. He envisioned a community with a new school." Mom added, "I thought this place would be perfect for Gary and you to grow up."

Mom continued, "I later learned the shingle siding was asbestos. The houses in the new development would be brick, a better choice now we know so much about asbestos." I did not want to change the subject by asking her about asbestos. I tried to keep the conversation happy. None of my friends seemed to have conversations with their moms. That may be why their moms liked me. I enjoyed talking with moms.

I believe this is what happened. Mr. Ladd looked at my mom, dressed in expensive clothes, high heels, and holding a genuine alligator leather purse. He decided to sell them a pricier house as they could afford it. Plus, Dad drove the expensive Buick to the site. Mr. Ladd could tell my parents knew excellence. I hear Mr. Ladd saying, "Wait just a bit and come see my new development in University City. It is called University Forest Estates." His ads in the newspaper called it "the talk of the town."

Taking Mr. Ladd's advice, Mom and Dad bought our house on the south side of Hazelwood Lane in this new "talk of the town" subdivision. I asked Mom how she chose our lot. "It was four lots away from the east end of Hazelwood Lane. The two corner lots, where the Brodskys and Marians lived, were oversized. Those backyards were visible from Partridge Avenue. I did not want people driving or walking down Partridge Avenue and looking into our backyard. We would have had to mow the side yard, which was not usable. It just added more space." The Brodskys later built a brick wall around their backyard for privacy. There was a mansion, my mansion, just on the other side of our street, the north side. I could see it from my front lawn.

Our new house had mansions surrounding it. There were two mansions just north of our house and one just across the street from my school. This last one was now a Catholic orphan home. The orphan home limestone mansion had a history of a mean owner, Theodore Salorgne, Jr. Mom told me, "I heard he inherited his wealth from his French Catholic father, who owned a buggy-and-carriage business downtown. The son married a woman named Agnes. They had a daughter, Josephine. Theodore Salorgne, Jr. abused his wife. After a miscarriage, a son was born. The son loved to ride horses. He died in his twenties when he was thrown from a horse while jumping a fence. Those are the stories I heard."

Mom could be a wealth of information. She continued, "Eventually, the Salorgne mansion was sold to German nuns, and the mansion became an orphanage." Children feared this mansion. Parents threatened to take their children to the orphanage for misbehaving. The orphan home was right across the street from my new school, University Forest Elementary School, which only went to the third grade when we moved into our home. The school district added six more classrooms and a gym just in time to save

Gary from going to Hawthorne Elementary, which was not within walking distance.

We did not have to drive to St. Louis City, University Hills, or Lewis Park to see mansions. Mansions were right in our neighborhood. Land, trees, and places to explore surrounded the mansions near me. My friend Mark and I walked over to a mansion on Faris Lane. He surprised me with this mansion. Later, I learned the Faris family built this mansion. It was as old as my mansion and once shared a family connection. It glistened all shiny white stone in the sunlight. God could have lived there. I still believed my dark stone mansion was better. The Faris mansion was torn down around 1959 to build a new street called Nixon Avenue. Tiny houses lined Nixon Avenue and replaced grandeur. Later, Mark told me, "A Russian spy lives in one of these houses."

"Were tiny houses going to replace all the mansions?" I asked Mark. He did not know. I feared for my mansion.

I could walk down this new street, Nixon Avenue, and see the carriage house of my mansion. I now regret I did not explore the Faris mansion more.

Chapter 3:
Eye, News, Costume, Indian

We visited furniture stores. We bought furniture. Gary and I played hide-and-seek among the furniture while my parents checked out various chairs, couches, and dining room sets. Mom poured over large books of fabrics, telling me, "I want silk fabric and no plastic covers on our furniture." They finally decided on a new dining room set. It was blond wood and had a matching cabinet designed by Eero Saarinen. I could not pronounce his name. Mom said, "He is famous. He won the competition to build the St. Louis Arch."

I was sitting in a Charles Eames chair Mom wanted. My parents decided our living room was too small for it. They purchased an octagon cocktail table made of pecan wood with iron supports between the top and bottom. It came with a matching bench, which ended up in front of our large picture window.

I especially liked the Stakmore folding card table and chair set. It was also blonde wood. The chair backs formed a leaf pattern, reminding me of pear tree leaves. I envisioned playing card games with friends, particularly Old Maid. Mom envisioned hosting Mah-Jongg with her lady friends. Dad wanted to use it as a poker table and to review his accounts.

Dad was looking at new cars. He bought one every three years. He traded the pink Buick for a turquoise-and-white Buick with fins. While Mom liked furniture, Dad and I liked cars. I knew all the models, including Buick, Pontiac, Chevrolet, Cadillac, and

Volkswagen, my favorite. I told Dad, "One day, I will own a red Volkswagen Beetle convertible." Dad smiled.

I started feeling guilty because the Beetle was Hitler's idea. Mom always said, "Living well is the best revenge." A Jewish girl who drove a bright red Beetle convertible. That is revenge.

It was about this time my parents became concerned about my lazy eye. It is an eye that does not have strong muscles and leans to the side. Mine leaned towards my nose. Mom said, "You inherited this from your father's family." We went to the eye doctor. We had to wait hours at Washington University's Eye Clinic. The eye doctor told us I needed surgery to correct the problem.

"What does that mean?" I asked.

"I shorten one of your eye muscles," he explained.

"You cut into my eye?"

"It is a common surgery."

"No one is going to cut into my eye."

Mom injected, "We have to correct the problem."

"No, no, no," I gave my final answer. Remember, I am four years old.

Hearing I did not agree to this, and Mom would not make me, the doctor explained I could see an optometrist. "The optometrist has an exercise program. The exercises may work to strengthen the eye muscles. You could try this therapy," he added.

"I want that," I told the doctor. Mom saw my willfulness. I realized I could make my own choices. I do not know what the doctor thought about a four-year-old making a serious medical decision. I am sure he told others about it.

Mom got the information and made the appointment. It was a long process. I had to wear a patch over my strong eye and do exercises to strengthen the muscles of my weak eye. I went to the optometrist's office to do eye exercises, looking at cartoons through a box. It worked! He told us the muscles might get weak again when I get older. "How old?"

"Oh, when you are an old lady." I was good to go.

I learned to speak up. Mom called it "advocating for myself." I could tell she was proud of me. I started moving my eyes from side to side to keep the muscles strong.

Dad read the *St. Louis Post-Dispatch* every night. He reported the daily news. "Here are the headlines. Jonas Salk's polio vaccine is declared safe and effective." That meant Gary and I would visit Dr. Cohen's office for polio shots. Gary heard me scream while I got my shot. He left the waiting room and walked home. Not a short walk. How did he find his way home? I am unsure how Mom convinced Gary to return to the doctor's office. Maybe she paid him. I got a pet turtle for getting my shot despite all my screaming.

Another evening, Dad told us about Rosa Parks, a Negro bus passenger. "She was arrested after refusing to give up her bus seat to a White passenger who was a man." We talked about her bravery. From Dad's nightly readings, we learned, "Emmett Till, a black fourteen-year-old teenager, was murdered for not showing respect to a White woman in Money, Mississippi."

"What did it mean not showing respect to a White woman?" I asked the question we were all thinking. No one knew. The world started to frighten me. My parents wanted me to know the world can be a scary place. La-la land does not exist. I wondered if Negros and Jews got along because some people hated both minorities. I remembered the phrase, *power in numbers*. If both minorities stick together, that could make them a majority or at least protect each other, I thought. I asked Dad about this idea. He said, "Both groups have experienced slavery, prejudice, ghetto living, and being hated."

There was good news, too. Dad reported, "Disney opened a big amusement park in California called Disneyland."

"I want to go. Can we go?" I asked. We had Kiddie Land down the street. "Maybe we can go to Holiday Hills? We pass it each time we drive to Uncle Louie and Aunt Evelyn's house."

"Tonight, we can all watch the first show of *Gunsmoke*. It is a new Western". Dad looked at me, "It's about cowboys." Dad's answer to Disneyland was a TV show.

"And Indians?" I asked.

"Probably," Dad answered.

I no longer thought about Disneyland, Kiddie Land, or Holiday Hills. I was thinking about Indians. I liked the clothes and jewelry Indians wore. I had an Indian costume our neighbor, Mrs. Brodsky, made for me. When I started school, I could wear the outfit to school on Halloween. Gary explained, "All the classes meet on the playground for Halloween. We form a line and walk around the playground showing everyone our costumes."

Meanwhile, I dressed in my Indian costume and played cowboys and Indians. It was a dress. I told myself I would wear it with corduroy pants underneath as I grew taller. I will save this costume for my daughter. I wore my turquoise Minnetonka moccasins with it.

Mrs. Brodsky designed the Indian costume from dark tan cotton canvas cloth. She sewed pieces of fur and beads on the front of the costume. It had fringe on the bottom and on the cuffs. She made necklaces from different-shaped noodles to look like animal bones and cut up colored straws for stones. I couldn't wait to start school and parade around the playground in my Indian costume. "I'm going to wear my Indian costume while we watch *Gunsmoke*."

The next day, I decided to wear my Indian outfit when I visited my mansion. I made friends with the cook, Mrs. McGee, and liked chatting with her while she cooked in the giant kitchen. Mrs. McGee lived at the mansion with her husband, two sons, and a dog. She reminded me of an Indian. She had black hair and tanned skin. I walked up the stairs to the kitchen as I usually did. Mrs. McGee stopped what she was doing and studied me. I broke the silence by telling her, "Mrs. Brodsky made this costume for me."

"I am an Indian. I am from the Quinault tribe. My tribe lived on the northwest coast by the Pacific Ocean. Stay here. I will be back." She left me alone in the kitchen. I did not move.

Mrs. McGee returned with a wooden box. She set it down on the counter in front of me. She opened the box and lifted the most beautiful silver and turquoise necklace. My first thought was Mom should see this. "This is real Indian jewelry. It was my mother's," she proudly stated.

"I have never seen anything so beautiful." Mrs. McGee let me hold the necklace. It was heavy.

She slipped the necklace over her head. It looked beautiful over her white apron. Then she lifted several bracelets from the box. "Here, try these on." My wrist was so skinny. The bracelets fit over my elbow. Each one was different.

"These stones are turquoise. Turquoise comes in different shades of blue and green. This stone is coral."

"I know this one." I touched a stone on a bracelet. "It is abalone. I have a large abalone shell in my collection." She nodded. As I left, she said, "I like your moccasins." I smiled and thanked her. While I walked home, I felt closer to Mrs. McGee. She shared her place and people with me.

Chapter 4:
More about the Brodskys

How was it growing up in a new neighborhood where a minority population was the majority? I could go on and on. About 98% living in University Forest Estates were Jewish. For now, I will talk about Christmas and Mrs. Brodsky. I need to introduce Mrs. Brodsky. She lived on the corner of our street. Hers was the first house on Hazelwood Lane, and ours was the fourth.

Mrs. Brodsky was an artist. She met her husband, Leslie, while studying dress design at Washington University. I don't know if she graduated. They got married in 1948. They had three boys. Monty, the oldest, was a year older than me. Randy was two years younger than me, and the youngest son was Paul. She called him Paul Paul. She came from a well-to-do family who lived on Cambridge Street in University City. The house was English Tudor, my favorite style home. Imagine Mom having a friend who majored in dress design. I wondered if they ever went dress shopping together. I lost track of Mrs. Brodsky after the fallout over me. Mom saw her name in the newspaper serving on various art committees.

No Christmas lights existed on Hazelwood Lane, Willow Tree Lane, White Oak Lane, or Faris Lane. I wondered if the few Christian neighbors who did not decorate their homes with lights did so out of respect for their Jewish neighbors. Mom drove me to Normandy, an area in North County, to see Christmas lights. It was now a Christian area. Mrs. Frank, our neighbor, was from Normandy. Later, her family moved to University City. Jews lived in Normandy at one time. Looking at these houses, I did not understand why Christians mounted wreaths on their doors. Weren't they just for graves in cemeteries? The two percent of non-Jewish people in our neighborhood did have Christmas trees positioned in the middle of the living room picture window. The Brodsky family was Jewish. Yet, they had a Christmas tree each year and invited my family to decorate it. Mom criticized the whole thing, but it was fun. "Jews do not have Christmas trees," she said.

However, we had Mom's family over for Christmas dinner and exchanged presents wrapped in Christmas paper. "We are just doing the fun part." Mom served ham with pineapple slices from a can and added a cherry to the center of each pineapple slice, attached by a toothpick. Even Dad ate the ham, and he grew up in a kosher home. Her Jell-O mold was layers of green and red. One year, she bought red felt and made a Christmas tablecloth. She agreed I could have a few glittery ornaments in the center of the table. Christmas was a national holiday, and one could not escape it. "Might as well join in the fun," Mom added.

Mom was Jewish but did not grow up in a religious home. She needed to learn Jewish history and customs in detail. Dad ensured we went to Sunday school, and Gary attended Hebrew school. I loved Sunday school. I learned about Abraham, Isaac, Jacob, Joseph, Moses, and their wives. There were famous women, Esther and Ruth. Ruth was my favorite. Dad and I watched a film about her, *The Story of Ruth*. It was about Jews keeping their land and working in wheat fields. My favorite part in the movie was when Ruth chose Boaz as her husband by lying down at his feet while he slept in a barley field. She took charge.

We celebrated all the traditional Jewish holidays. Rosh Hashanah and Yom Kippur were called High Holidays. For Rosh Hashanah, Gary and I stayed home from school. We went to Shaare Zedek Synagogue. Mom bought me a red wool suit and a white hat with red roses. She always looked spectacular. We both did. Rabbi Epstein kissed us both a happy new year. We felt he liked us best. Sometimes, The Rabbi invited Dad to recite a prayer. It was an honor. The next holiday was Yom Kippur, the Day of Atonement. It was a solemn day devoted to fasting, prayer, and repentance. I tried to fast, but I could not. I was starving even when I ate. Dad was the only one who could fast all day. I respected this holiday. The holiday required people to ask for forgiveness from those offended. It made sense. I'll write down offenses to remember them over the year. During these two holidays, all the Jewish kids stayed home from school. Only three or four Christian students attended each class during the Jewish holidays. Teachers showed movies, did art projects, and sang songs. The school extended recess. I asked Mom, "Why don't they close the school?"

"It's a public school," Mom answered. "They have to stay open."

In University City, everything closed during these holidays, except for the main grocery stores or other businesses owned by Gentiles, non-Jews. Dad's store closed because a Jew owned the business, and Jews worked there. For Hanukkah, we did not miss school. We had a traditional menorah. Plus, Mom bought a menorah she plugged into a socket to light up. She placed it in our picture window. Christmas and Hanukkah sometimes overlapped in December. I preferred the simplicity of Hanukkah. It celebrated how Jews won a war against the Greeks and Syrians. They did not want us to practice our religion. Judah Maccabee was a war hero and saved our temple. We ate potato pancakes, called latkes, with sour cream and apple sauce. We received a silver dollar each night for a week. I mistakenly deposited the silver dollars in my bank account instead of holding onto them in a safety deposit box. Each silver dollar would be worth more money in the future. I understood a theme in most Jewish holidays. We celebrated survival.

I felt sorry for all the poor children who would not get a present for Christmas. It could be a sad holiday for children and stressful for parents. Only those with money could celebrate all the "pomp and circumstance," as Mom called it. Before Christmas, Mom read the "100 Neediest Cases" published in the newspaper to Gary and me.

"Everyone deserves a Christmas present," Mom told us.

Gary and I picked a case. We donated a dollar each. We chose this year:

Wilma is a single mother of 5 children, Athena 15, Isaiah 7, John 10, Flora 7 and Christian 11. She is unemployed and they live in public housing. Wilma is looking for work but currently her only income is child support when it comes. Her children are her everything, she has a songbird, a football player, basketball player, and pianist. Her mother helps when she can. It would be a blessing to see her children happy for Christmas. Items needed: Department store gift certificates, coats, boots, utility payments, toys.

Mom told me a story. When she was young, she asked her mom, "What am I getting for Christmas?"

Her mom (my Grandma Bertha) told her to close her eyes. Grandma Bertha asked, "What do you see?"

"Nothing," Mom responded.

"That is what you are getting," my Grandma Bertha answered. Mean. I believed Mom wanted Gary and me to donate to the "100 Neediest Cases" so other children would not experience an unhappy Christmas. She tried to teach us to be kind. Later, I tried buying Mom something special for her birthdays and other holidays to compensate for her mom's meanness. The wounds lasted forever.

Back to Mrs. Brodsky and decorating the Christmas tree. She bought beautiful colored glass ornaments. I felt like I was putting jewelry on a tree. When we finished placing the ornaments on the tree, she handed out the silver tinsel. I loved all the glitter. Finally, she made fake snow and threw it all over the tree. I preferred the tree with just the glitter. The pretend snow hid the glitter. Our families celebrated Christmas together for three years before the relationship ended. I was the center of all the conflicts and the eventual fallout.

The first red flag occurred when Mrs. Brodsky visited our house one evening. There were three houses between our homes. She walked over. She dressed like a beatnik: black stretch pants, a black turtleneck, a black beret, and black flat pointed shoes. Her trademark was her thick, black-rimmed glasses. Mom was the opposite. She always wore pointy high heels and lots of bright colors. Mom's trademark was a pair of glittery gold-framed sunglasses. Mrs. Brodsky and Mom were sitting on the new couches.

"Beautiful furnishings," Mrs. Brodsky complimented Mom. Mom beamed. Mrs. Brodsky's comment was meaningful because Mrs. Brodsky was an artist, and her husband owned a furniture store. I was happy she came over to visit. I decided to sing "Somewhere Over the Rainbow." Mrs. Brodsky and her kids watched *The Wizard of Oz* with Mom, Gary, and me. I cried when the evil woman seized Toto. Mom carried me to the lobby, where we stayed until I calmed down.

I wanted to impress Mrs. Brodsky. After my performance, Mrs. Brodsky got up from the couch and ran over to me. I thought she was going to hug and kiss me. Instead, she pulled my pants down and bit me hard on my butt cheek. I screamed, and then I cried. Mom was shocked. "She is so cute. I could not help myself. I am sorry." She looked at me, "I did not mean to hurt you." She left. Her teeth marks stayed.

"Do I need a rabies shot?" It was one of those moments when parents must not laugh at a four-year-old's question because the situation is serious. Mom applied Vaseline.

That incident did not end the friendship. The end came two years later when Mrs. Brodsky told Mom, "I will pick Linda up from the Varsity Theatre." Mom had someplace she needed to go. Mom dropped me off at the theater.

"You know Mrs. Brodsky's car?"

"Yes. It is the big station wagon with the fake wood on the sides."

"Don't get into the car unless she is the driver."

The theater was safe back then. I knew not to go anywhere with a stranger. I sat by myself. I saw *Old Yeller* and *The

Incredible Shrinking Man. I ate chocolate Turkish taffy and cried silently when Old Yeller died.

Mom arrived at Mrs. Brodsky's house later that day to pick me up. Mrs. Brodsky cried out, "Oh no, I forgot to pick her up!"

"You what?" No time to fight now. Mom ran out of Mrs. Brodsky's house in her high heels and jumped back into her black, 1953, deluxe two-door Chevrolet known as Betsy. She drove the two miles to the Varsity Theatre fast. I stayed outside the Varsity Theatre, waiting for Mrs. Brodsky as the sun descended on Delmar Avenue. I walked up and down the street a little bit to keep warm. Then it started to rain. Cars with blinding lights drove by me.

Never again, Mom thought as she drove to find me. Mom found me standing on Delmar Avenue in the dark. I recognized Betsy as Mom pulled up to the curb by the Varsity Theatre.

"Anything could have happened. She's unpredictable." Mom kept repeating this on the way home. I was relieved to be in Mom's warm car and kept quiet. I wanted to bring up getting a dog. I realized the opportunity was ruined by Mrs. Brodsky upsetting Mom. Mom called Mrs. Brodsky as soon as we got home. "Don't ever speak to me or my family again," Mom screamed through the telephone. Mom turned to me, "Don't speak to any of the Brodsky family."

I understood why I was not allowed to go over there anymore. I was still intrigued by Mrs. Brodsky's artistic talents. I missed her. I missed exploring her magic closet in the basement of her home. There she had boxes of glittery items aside from Christmas ornaments and art supplies. Now, just walking by her house scared me. They painted their house a dark gray, almost black. They added a high brick wall around the backyard so no one could see into it. They had a large pine tree on the front lawn, one of the original trees on the land. At night, I thought it was a giant tarantula from the movie *Tarantula*. Mrs. Brodsky was not the best mother. She did weird stuff, Mom told me.

Her oldest son Monty taught me to pick my friends wisely. Here is what happened. I was outside, exploring near where he stood. He walked over to a neighbor's barking dog, and he peed on the dog. The dog's owner recognized him and called Mrs. Brodsky. The dog owner identified me as being at the crime scene. The dog owner asked Mrs. Brodsky for Mom's telephone number.

Mom questioned me about it. "I was there. I saw him pee on the dog. Why be mean to the dog? Monty was on their lawn, and the dog was protecting it." I started to cry. I now understood my mother's decision to end contact with the whole family. I understood the words "mean," "weird," and "crazy," which Mom used to describe Monty and Mrs. Brodsky. Mr. and Mrs. Brodsky moved. Later, they divorced. Sometimes, we are attracted to people because they are talented, fun, imaginative, or engaging. Other characteristics, such as kindness and a moral compass, are missing. Lesson: Some bad people can be attractive. Stay away.

Chapter 5:
Are There Rules?

My first week in kindergarten proved problematic. The school assigned me to afternoon kindergarten. That meant I could hang out with Mom in the mornings. I lived a block away from school. Being five years old and walking alone to school was natural. It was safe in our neighborhood. I waved to Mrs. Daniels, our crosswalk guard. Since I lived on the same side of the street as the school, I did not need her help. I only had to cross Willow Tree Lane, a street like mine. When I got to school early, I could play on the playground till school started. A bell would ring to let everyone know it was time to quit whatever they were doing and go directly to class. Then another bell rang. Everyone was seated in their chairs except me. No one explained this to me. While daydreaming, I just stayed outside and wandered into kindergarten class when I was ready. Mom received a phone call from the school. It came from the principal, Mr. Barnard. "What?" my mom asked. "How can that be? She leaves the house early enough to get there." I explained I did not know I had to be there at a specific time.

"Where did you think all the children were going when the bell rang?"

"I don't know. I play at the big playground with Charlene Ponstingl." (She was Gary's friend). "When she goes to class, I go to the kindergarten playground. No one is there, and I have it all to myself." I was starting a pattern of enjoying my own company.

"Here is how this works," Mom said. "When the bell rings, go to class. When Charlene goes to class, you go to class, too."

"Ok, I understand." I was never late to school or anything else again.

One day before school, Peggy and I picked flowers for our teacher. "Yes, we went into people's yards and picked flowers," I confessed to my teacher.

"That is stealing." I was horrified. How did I know I was stealing? "It was my idea." I got Peggy in trouble by asking her to go with me. I learned I could not go into neighbors' backyards and pick flowers from their gardens without permission.

What were the rules in general? Politeness. One day, I heard a classmate say "fuck" on the playground. I came home and asked Mom, "What does fuck mean?" I must have pronounced it right because she almost slapped me after I said the word.

She caught herself and asked, "Where did you hear that?"

"A classmate." I did not want to get him in trouble.

"It is the worst word in our language. Do not repeat it."

"What does it mean?"

"You are too young to understand now."

The word scared me. I learned words can be scary.

The *Ten Commandments* were the rules. Examples were no telling lies, no stealing, no cheating, no hitting another person, the basics. I did hit my neighbor, Lisa. She was at my house, and we were playing. I asked her a question, and she did not, could not, or would not reply. "If you do not answer me, I am going to hit you over the head with this gun" (a toy gun). She kept silent. I followed through with my promise and hit her. I got into a lot of trouble. Mom put ice on Lisa's head and called her mom. I was about three years old, and she was two. Maybe she did not understand me. I was grateful Lisa's mom did not call the police. I feared punishment. Punishment meant staying at the orphan home down the street or going to jail. We did not have the term, grounded back then.

I remember going to a friend's house just as dinner ended. My friend could not leave the table until she ate everything on her plate. My parents never forced me to eat anything. I was grateful these were not my parents and my rules.

My parents said, "Just do the right thing." Simple. I was surprised to find other kids lying, stealing, and being mean to other schoolmates. We had to memorize the *Ten Commandments* for Sunday school. I did take the Lord's name in vain. It happened while I was showing Blackie my butterfly. I yelled, "Goddammit, Blackie Fine. You son-of-a-bitch. You ate my butterfly." It was a warm summer day. All the neighbors' windows were open. When Mom heard me scream these obscenities, she came running outside. I explained the situation. "Dad says goddammit all the time." He learned those words in the army. I was confused. Mom was going to tell Dad not to cuss.

There were times when I was jealous or wanted what someone else had. Not material things but talents, brains, and athleticism. A few of the *Ten Commandments* I disobeyed. These were sins I outgrew.

Chapter 6:
Reality of First Grade

Miss Ayers and I duked it out. A battle raged between a six-year-old and a first-grade teacher who served in the armed forces. Mom told me, "I heard Miss Ayers responded to President Truman's call for service in 1951. President Truman needed to build the military and considered it necessary women voluntarily serve."

"What did she do in the military?" Mom did not know. I could have asked Miss Ayers while we were alone after school. I was writing 100 times on the board not to do something. That was the only time we were alone together. She realized it would take me a long time to write whatever I did wrong 100 times. After 20 minutes, she decided I could go home. Miss Ayers punished me long enough. To me, she was mean and strict. My parents failed to explain the seriousness of school. How could I be confined to a chair all day? I am an explorer. It defeated independence. I squirmed in my desk chair. Miss Ayers told me to sit still.

Wearing pants to school started another battle. Mom bought me two new outfits. They both consisted of flannel plaid shirts and corduroy pants, each lined in the flannel of the matching shirt: boys' clothes. They were instant favorites I wanted to wear to school. I dressed in one outfit.

"Girls can't wear pants to school. Girls wear dresses with pants underneath when it is cold," Mom explained.

"I cannot ruin this by putting a skirt over the pants."

My mother knew it was hopeless to argue with me. We were both fashion icons. She ignored the situation and let me attend school in my new cowboy clothes, or maybe they were lumberjack clothes. Everyone stared as I took my seat. Miss Ayres walked over and told me to put my skirt over the pants.

"I am not wearing a skirt today." She does not know about fashion, I thought to myself.

Miss Ayers walked to her desk, wrote something on paper, folded it, and placed it in an envelope. Then she sealed the envelope. She approached me, holding the envelope and a giant safety pin.

Here it comes, the note.

She pinned the envelope to my new flannel shirt. I wore the envelope all day. I hope it does not make a hole in my shirt. When I returned home, my mom opened the safety pin, removed the envelope, opened it, and read the note.

Dear Mrs. Fine,

Linda was dressed inappropriately for school today. The University Forest Elementary School requires all girls to wear skirts or dresses. Girls may wear pants under a skirt or dress. Girls are allowed to do this for gym class and if it is cold outside for recess. Be sure she follows the rules. Thank you,

Sincerely,

Miss Ayers

I believed my mom was wise to let the school resolve the situation. That settled that. I hated rules that made no sense.

We had to take the IQ test. Miss Ayers told us it stood for Intelligence Quotient. "It helps the school know how well you learn." She gave each student an answer sheet and a booklet filled with questions. We received strict instructions on how to fill in the answers. Miss Ayers explained, "Do not go outside of the circle with your pencil. Be sure to fill the whole circle." Each test was timed. I focused on filling in the circles correctly. Miss Ayers warned the class that our time was almost up. I had a lot more questions to read and circles to complete. I filled in the remaining circles without reading the questions. I created patterns with my answers as I finished the test.

Miss Ayers called Mom for a meeting after school. I was to be there too. Miss Ayers started by saying she thought I was smart. "However, Linda does not pay attention in class." She showed Mom my scores on the IQ tests. The scores showed I was not intelligent.

Mom turned to me. "Can you explain this?"

"I was making patterns on the answer sheet. And I was confused by the pictures of what is right and left. I do not know what that means." Mom could see she needed to teach me the basics. Too much time spent chatting about other things, she thought to herself. Gary did not have these problems.

Miss Ayers told us I could retake the IQ test. She would arrange it.

"Thank you so much, Miss Ayers," Mom said. Mom drove us home. "That was nice of Miss Ayers." I sat there dreading this redo.

The next battle with Miss Ayers was principle-based. After World War II, nothing went to waste, especially food. Adults told children that other children around the world were starving. Adults lectured, "You must eat all your food." I believed this was silly. If I had leftover food, the food would not travel to Europe or elsewhere to help starving children. I did not know Mom and everyone rationed food during World War II. Parents did not educate us about the food shortages worldwide and in our city. Most parents protected their children from World War II's horrors even though parents were severely affected. The following story illustrates strong beliefs and misunderstandings.

My true uniqueness started at my favorite place, the St. Louis Zoo. Almost every Saturday, Mom drove me to the zoo. We entered the Primate House. I called it the Monkey House. There at the entrance was Phil the Gorilla. He came to the zoo after being captured in Africa in 1941. He died in 1958. I was seven years old when Phil died. Phil changed my life. I stood in front of Phil, and I asked Mom, "Do people eat gorillas?"

Mom was surprised by my question. I was only five years old. She was not sure how to answer. "I suppose in some places, people eat gorillas." It seemed a safe answer. What followed was mayhem.

"Phil looks like me. He looks like a person. How can people eat an animal that looks like a person? How do people decide what animals are OK to eat?"

"I do not know," Mom confessed.

"That's it. I am not going to eat any animals, no meat."

"You must eat meat. You will die if you do not eat meat."

"Then I will die," I proclaimed. I kept my word. No meat. Especially, no chicken. Birds were my favorite. Seeing a chicken with its feathers plucked upset me. Not only did I not eat meat, but I also rejected any food that touched meat. When my mom cooked chicken, I left the kitchen. The sight of raw chicken made me sick. I lost weight, got too thin, protein deprived. Cousin Sam told Mom to go to the health food store and buy meat substitutes, beans made to look like meat. She did not follow through, and I got skinnier.

Back to Miss Ayers. Miss Ayers and I had minor skirmishes. The school cafeteria turned into a battleground. My usual lunch was peanut butter and Welch's grape jelly sandwich on Wonder Bread. Mom never put enough peanut butter on the bread, and I found it smashed by lunchtime. One day, we must have been out of one of the ingredients because I had to buy my lunch. Standing in the lunch line, I became anxious. To my horror, they served roast beef smothered in gravy, mashed potatoes, and green beans. I should have told the cafeteria lady to hold the roast beef, but it was too late. She handed me the plate. I walked to a table, sat down, and ate the potatoes and green beans. I got up from the table to return my tray. Walking across the cafeteria, Miss Ayers spotted me. "Young lady, sit back down and eat that roast beef. You cannot leave the cafeteria until you have eaten your lunch."

I told Miss Ayers that I was a vegetarian. "Vegetarians do not eat meat."

"I never heard of such a thing. Take your tray back to the table." She repeated the argument about people elsewhere starving.

I walked over to the table and sat down. I came up with a plan. I waved Charlene Ponstingl over to where I was sitting. Remember, she was three years older than me and a friend of my brother. I explained my situation. I talked fast, "When Miss Ayers is not looking, take my tray back. I'll run away."

She agreed to help me. I ran away from school. Unfortunately, Mom was not home. I did not have a key to my house. Remember,

I am six years old. I crossed the street to Mrs. Alper's house. She invited me in. She contacted the school to tell the principal I was safe. I am sure Miss Ayers was concerned I disappeared after lunch, not sitting at my desk with my hands folded. Mrs. Alper told the principal, "There was a problem at lunchtime. Linda ran away. Linda will be staying with me until her mom arrives home." Mrs. Alper and I waited for Mom to come home. We sat in lawn chairs on her driveway. The black Chevy pulled up to the front of my house, and we crossed the street to greet Mom.

"Hi, Bess. Linda ran away from school because Miss Ayers was trying to make her eat meat. I called the school, and they know she is with me." I filled in the dramatic details.

Mom gratefully said, "Thank you for taking care of Linda."

"Thank you, Mrs. Alper. Bye, Frisky." Frisky was the Alper's dog. Mrs. Alper always appeared when I was in a crisis.

Livid, Mom and I walked into the principal's office together. The principal called Miss Ayers to his office. Mom explained the situation endangered me. It forced me to run away. "She could have been killed crossing the street or kidnapped." Kidnapped was her go-to. She cited a list of dangerous outcomes. Mom turned to Miss Ayers, "You should have listened to what Linda was telling you."

Miss Ayers learned a new term, *vegetarian*. At the end of first grade, I discovered the importance of sticking up for myself. I also learned sometimes I must do what I am told. I never found out what Miss Ayers did during her military service to protect our country. When we parted, I admired and respected her as my teacher.

Chapter 7:
Blackie, My Mansion, and a New Book

Mom worked part-time, and I found myself with unimaginable freedom. Arriving home from school, I planned my explorations. Sometimes, Gary walked over to my mansion with me. We explored the grounds together. We found insects that looked like leaves and others that looked like sticks. I searched for furry caterpillars. My favorite find was the Luna moth. I brought one home and kept it inside our screened-in porch. Another Luna moth showed up on the outside of the porch. I figured they were mates. I let the moth inside the porch free so they were together again.

Mom read me every newspaper story about kidnappings. Then one of my classmates, Barb, was almost kidnapped. She was walking on her street, Plymouth Avenue. A man pulled his car up to her and invited her inside. She screamed and ran home. This news traveled quickly to everyone attending University Forest Elementary School. I wondered if the police ever caught him. I started leaving notes at home telling Mom where I was going. Just in case the police needed to know my last whereabouts.

I could not resist visiting my mansion. My mansion was the name I gave this century-old, limestone, fourteen-room estate. You will hear about my mansion's history and its prominent owners. But not now. I am on my way there to visit Mrs. McGee, the cook.

I found a three-legged turtle before I reached the mansion steps and took it home. I found Mom's pink nail polish and painted my name on the turtle's shell. I hope the nail polish did not hurt the turtle. I carried it back to my mansion. I wanted to keep the turtle in his familiar place. It might have a mate. My name protected the turtle. Samuel McGee, who lived in the mansion, told me he saw the three-legged turtle with my name. Samuel was the son of the cook and groundskeeper. I later studied box turtles at the library. They spend their lives in a small area. If removed from their familiar home, they will die. I thought about Dad's family moving from Lithuania. Unlike turtles, they prospered in their new place.

On this visit, the school was still in session. I hoped to see Mrs. McGee's dog, Blackie. Remember, my mansion was a two-minute walk from my house. Boldly, I walked up the outside steps onto the wrap-around porch, opened the front door, and walked over to the stairs on the side of the spacious entryway. Walnut wood was on the walls and made up the decorative stairs and railing. My mansion resembled the mansions in the movies I watched on the *Early Show*. It was a *Meet Me in St. Louis* movie mansion. Only bigger. The imposing stairs were not easy to climb for someone my size. The huge kitchen was on the second floor.

I found Mrs. McGee cooking. This boarding school, called St. Louis Junior Academy of Science, a Seventh-Day Adventist private school, was my true oyster. My neighborhood and the rest of University City were my kosher oyster. Copper pots lined the walls. That must be why I love copper. Everything was out in the open. Easy to grab. Mrs. McGee cooked for the students, faculty, and all living there.

She offered me an oatmeal cookie she just baked. There was Blackie sitting on the floor, looking tired. Mrs. McGee and I visited a lot. Remember, I enjoyed the company of adults. "I saw the movie *Old Yeller*. It is about a dog and a boy. I want to be a girl and her dog." I wondered if her sons went to see movies.

She responded, "Blackie is pregnant." I got excited. Then doubt set in.

"I had Vicky's puppy for a short time, a few days. The puppy peed in my doll buggy. I returned the puppy to Mrs. Frank. It was a few years ago."

"You are older now. Seven years old is a better age for a puppy. Talk to your parents."

She boosted my confidence. I needed someone to teach me how to be a dog mom. My parents never had a dog. Mrs. Frank had moved. My best friend's mom, Mrs. Townsend, came to mind.

About two months later, when I visited Mrs. McGee, Blackie had her puppies. I wanted the puppy that looked most like Blackie, the mother. The mom was a cocker spaniel. The breed of the dad was unknown. I thought about the dogs in the neighborhood for possible dog dads. I hoped it was not the Swartz's dog. We were all afraid of Swartz's dog, a large German shepherd. The litter had an all-black male puppy. He was going to be my Blackie. Mom bought all the dog items I needed. I carried my Blackie home. When my Blackie was a little older, we ran to my mansion (Blackie never walked), exploring together.

Then one day, it all came to a halt. I came to visit Mrs. McGee. She explained, "The reverend and headmaster told me to tell you this is private property. They said you are trespassing. You cannot visit this school anymore. It is only for the students and their families." I felt crushed. She was sorry. What could I say? I did not think about trespassing issues. I did have nightmares about the mansion. Someone was trying to hang me on the mansion's arbor. I woke up screaming. I was prone to nightmares. I even dreamt Mom was trying to kill me by stabbing me. I wanted Blackie to sleep in my room for protection. My parents denied this request.

The next day after school, I greeted Blackie in the yard. I wondered if he was sad about not going to see his mom anymore. He was so happy to see me. We visited.

I decided to read. I had another orange book to finish and return to the library. It was about Mary Queen of Scots. "You will not like the ending," Mom warned me when she saw the book earlier. I headed into the living room to read. Poor Mary, the beginning of her life was not happy. Mary was six days old when her father died, and she inherited the throne. The story was filled with Mary moving to several countries, having numerous marriages, and being a threat to Queen Elizabeth. I was shocked to read Queen Elizabeth ordered Mary beheaded because Mary threatened Elizabeth's crown. Mom was right. I protested the ending. I decided to take Blackie for a run to stop thinking about Mary.

Running back towards the house, I saw Mom's car, Betsy, parked in front of our home. I returned Blackie to the backyard. Then I walked into the kitchen. Mom had a smile on her face. I told her about my day. I was sad about Mary Queen of Scots. "I hope I do not have a nightmare about her."

Mom changed the subject. "Aside from Shakespeare, Louisa May Alcott is my favorite writer," she told me.

"What did she write?"

Mom started walking towards my bedroom. "Follow me." On my bed was a wrapped box. Stix, Baer, and Fuller gift-wrapped the present. Everything about the package was unique and beautiful. I was so surprised. I approached it carefully and gently opened the box. I found a thick hardback book with a cover showing girls from another time in history standing around a piano. A girl with long hair was playing the piano. "They are sisters," Mom said. I could hear the excitement in her voice. The sisters wore clothes from the 1800s, and the room reminded me of a room in my mansion. I loved it already.

I read the title, "*Little Women* by Louisa May Alcott." It was the most beautiful book I had ever seen. I gave Mom a hug and kiss. I settled in the living room on the couch, turned on the pole lamp, and started reading. I met Jo. Jo became my inspiration. That night when Mom tucked me in and kissed me goodnight, I told her how much I loved the new book. She told me it was her favorite, too. "Who is your favorite character?" I asked her.

"Beth," she said. "Beth was kind." I was surprised. I thought Mom would choose Amy. Amy was fashionable and loved beautiful clothes.

"I like Jo. She wore pants and wanted to write books. Jo was outspoken, smart, and independent."

Later, I realized Mom needed a Beth. Mom grew up in a house where kindness was lacking. Maybe Mom learned how to be kind by reading about Beth's compassionate acts.

Chapter 8:
I Went Too Far

In 1958 everything was good. I was in second grade. I had my best friend, Janice Townsend, in my class. I had my grasshopper, Peanuts. He came to school with me every day in a jar. Plus, I had Nicky Bird, a parakeet living in my bedroom. Life was great. My teacher was an older woman, Mrs. Long. She had white hair like my Bubba. She taught handwriting mainly and how to take care of geraniums. She had about ten clay pots, each filled with geraniums, lining the windows. She told me about deadheading the plants. "This will bring new healthy flowers." A few times, she let me deadhead the plants.

I sat parallel to the windows, which was dangerous because I was distracted by every bird flying by or landing on the telephone wires. While in class, I learned to identify the songs of blue jays, cardinals, starlings, and robins. Now, I knew the bird's species without having to find the bird in a tall tree. I knew a cardinal in flight by its flying pattern. However, I did not know where the class was reading in the book. When it was my turn to read out loud, I searched for the right place. Because of a delay, Mrs. Long believed I did not know how to read. She placed me in an impaired reading group.

Mom talked to Mrs. Long to sort it out. "Linda reads the children's classics at home. She reads the orange biography books from the library." Teachers did not know about attention deficit disorders. "Earth to Linda," my friends would say. After Mom talked with Mrs. Long, I transferred to a more advanced reading group. Mom warned me to pay attention.

I conquered a fear. The fear was climbing the rope in gym class. Mr. Deardorff attached a rope to the ceiling of the gym. Once a month, we took turns climbing the rope to the ceiling. Some of us dreaded this monthly torture. Just about all the boys could achieve the "Hip hip hoorays" given to those who could touch the top. I wanted to do this. I started lifting the weights my parents bought for Gary to build up my weak vegetarian arms. It worked. I heard the cheers from my classmates, "Hip hip hooray." These were the only cheers I received in gym class, ever.

For some, this idyllic period ended during bomb shelter drills, where we ran to the school hallway, got down on our knees with hands clasped over our heads, and waited to hear the all-clear. For me, this idyllic period ended when Mr. Deardorff, the gym teacher, introduced us to National Youth Fitness Week. I learned I was the slowest runner in my class, maybe in the whole school. Imagine my humiliation when Mr. Deardorff posted the scores for the 50-yard dash on the classroom wall. Barry announced to everyone I was the slowest runner. It was the first time I experienced humiliation. Not even my ballet teacher could humiliate me like this.

Janice must have said something to her dad. Mr. Townsend drove Janice and me to Heman Park. We trained for the upcoming 600-yard dash. The training helped. My lungs were on fire, but at least I was not last to cross the finish line. I achieved the max of fifty sit-ups and took pride in the accomplishment even though my stomach ached for several days afterward. I did not have skills, just determination.

My dance teacher was Carmen Thomas. Yes, the famous Carmen Thomas, who danced with the Radio City Rockettes in New York City. It is a problem when parents can afford the best. Mom sent me to the best dancing school in St. Louis, Carmen Thomas Studio. I was the stiffest child ever born, a new revelation. I later realized Mom enrolled me in ballet, thinking it would help me in gym class and maybe in life. Mom read ballet could improve concentration, build physical strength, and increase flexibility. I needed ballet.

It started like this. When Miss Thomas saw my stiffness, she started cranking on my joints to stretch me. Had she known yoga, she could have taught me some poses to increase my joint range gently. Instead, she chose to torture me. "This is not going to work," I told my mom.

"Do you enjoy tap dancing?"

"Yes, tap dancing is fun." We danced to my favorite songs: "Bye Bye Blackbird" and "When the Red Red Robin Comes Bob Bob Bobbin Along". I liked these songs because they were about my neighborhood birds.

Mom called the dance school and canceled my ballet lessons. Then things got worse. During a tap dance lesson, I had to go to the bathroom. Miss Thomas told me I could not go. I told her, "I have to use the bathroom."

"No."

"If you do not let me, I will pee in my pants."

"No."

She left me no choice. To everyone's surprise, and probably horror, I peed in my black leotard.

"Go into the bathroom and clean yourself up. Wear your undershirt and underpants to dance in. Clean this mess up."

I did as she said. I tap danced in my underwear.

I explained what had happened to Mom. Mom told Miss Thomas, "Linda will not return after the recital." Miss Thomas had a waiting list. She was glad to know I was leaving. We finished the season because I already had my purple-and-salmon satin costume handmade by Miss Thomas' seamstress. Then there were those two favorite songs.

The recital was fabulous. I danced at the famous Fox Theatre. "I am proud of you," Dad said in the car on the way home. I started regretting my rebellion. I did have to use the bathroom.

Later, I took dancing lessons with Janice. We went to a basement studio built in a woman's house. Our recital costumes were our black leotard with a silly skunk tail attached and a headband with fake skunk ears. It was not Carmen Thomas style, but fun. I only danced there for one season. I missed the Fox Theatre and the satin.

Chapter 9:
With My Mom

Mom and I started the day at the University City Firehouse, where residents who collected money for the American Heart Association would turn in donations. Mom was the volunteer coordinator who counted all money and then sent it to the national charity. Mom offered her help to pay God back for saving Gary. He was born with a hole in his heart.

Our family friend, Mr. Hewitt, worked as a fireman, and we visited with him. He brought Mom a cup of coffee. It was winter and cold in the firehouse garage, where we waited for people to turn in donations. I left my coat on the whole time we were there. Later, I walked across Olive Street Road to Hamburger Heaven for French fries with hot sauce and a Coke. I felt grown up crossing the busy street by myself, entering the kitchen, placing my food order, and paying for it. With my carryout, I hurried back to the firehouse so Mom would not worry, though I did consider running over to Pennsylvania Food Shop for penny candy. I craved Turkish Taffy.

"Did you leave a tip?"

"Yes, ten cents," I proudly replied. "The bill was only fifty-five cents."

University City residents understood the city's uniqueness. We saw residential street signs named Harvard, Yale, Princeton, Cornell, Stanford, and Dartmouth, to name a few, reminding residents of the importance of education. Children felt the grandeur of their city, bordering Washington University, home to the 1904 World's Fair. The founder, Edward Gardner Lewis, built University City as a place for art, literacy, education, and freedom to excel. Lewis commissioned the impressive Lion Gates, also known as the Gates of Opportunity, in the early 1900s.

Let me explain. On either side of Delmar Boulevard, just west of the commercial district called the Loop, stand the gatekeepers to University City. The gatekeepers were two massive feline figures perched on their 40-foot limestone mounts. They kept watch high above the heads of pedestrians and motorists. These lions were two of the only structures visible for miles when University City transformed from acres of pastureland to mansions for the wealthy. Lewis decided giant lions should guard the entrance to his dream city. He hired Thomas Young of Eames and Young Architects to design the 40-foot limestone mounts. Lewis commissioned the artist George Julian Zolnay to create the monolithic lion and lioness.

There is more to brag about. My stately junior high school, Hanley Junior High School, was the first junior high school in the country. The senior high school embodied a grand prep-school environment. Everywhere, I saw symbols telling me to strive for excellence. Just about everyone attending my school, University Forest Elementary School, excelled in their education. I felt smart living here.

Feeling safe was most important to parents and grandparents. Occasionally, I saw a person with a number tattooed on the arm. It was a reminder of Hitler.

A neighbor, Diane, was lucky to have her grandparents live down the street. She could visit them anytime. My grandmothers were a car ride away. I still felt blessed. Some of my classmates lost grandparents in the war. We looked for reassurance. Being surrounded by Jewish people, stores, delicatessens, synagogues, and symbols brought a sense of security. We felt comfortable, and our environment was predictable. The regular grocery store, National Food Store, had a whole aisle of Jewish foods for Passover. It was an ideal place.

One time, Dad interrupted a chat about University City being a perfect world by saying, "Jews never feel safe."

"But we are safe here?"

"For now," Dad said. "We keep moving. Our history is traveling to a new place because we get kicked out of our current place that we made great just so someone else can take it over." I had never heard Dad talk like this before. He was always so optimistic. Mom, the realist would have said that. Then I remembered Dad experienced persecution as a boy in Lithuania. I wondered if our house would be my family's forever home.

My dad, Hyman, left Lithuania as a young boy. The czar gave orders to attack and burn Jewish villages. Sometimes it was soldiers who attacked. Sometimes it was the police. Sometimes it was hoodlums. Dad's father, my grandfather Joseph (*Zahdah*, Yiddish for grandfather), left first with my Aunt Bess. My brave grandmother, Hilda (*Bubba* to me, Yiddish for grandmother), traveled with her two sons from Lithuania to Japan and finally to the West Coast of the United States by ship. They landed in the United States in 1917, a dangerous year. They traveled by train across the United States to St. Louis, Missouri. None of them spoke English. They spoke Yiddish and Hebrew. Dad had not seen his father and sister for four years. I am not sure my mother understood all this. Dad lived through horrific times as a child.

Dad had to adjust to a new country, language, and culture. Yet he seemed happy to me. He always whistled. Dad's whistling was a sign the house was in a happy moment.

After World War II, White men who served in the United States armed forces, like Dad, bought their homes on loans from the GI Bill. I learned it was harder for Negros to get the same benefits entitled to them. Mom lamented she wished Dad had taken advantage of the educational opportunities from the GI Bill. He quit school after eighth grade to work. His parents needed financial help.

"Who has their son quit school?" She asked me this question again and again. I resented these negative comments. I loved my grandparents. They were remarkable given the circumstances, coming from an oppressive, murderous place, and traveling across the world to the unknown. I learned not to disagree with Mom. She got mad.

Instead, I said, "I want to work." That changed the subject. I understood work meant freedom. Louisa May Alcott, my role model, was a workaholic. I am going to be a workaholic, too, and do things.

Mom was still thinking about Dad not going to college. "Educated people, people who attend college, earn more money," she explained.

"I will work to pay for college." I thought that would make her happy. She voiced other plans.

"Attend secretarial school, work for a law firm, and marry one of the lawyers."

I thought, no way. To sit in front of a typewriter all day sounded boring. Like Jo in *Little Women*, I wanted to type my words, not someone else's. I related to Jo. I daydreamed about being Jo. I wondered why Mom's goals for me were so passive.

"I was smart enough to go to college and succeed. I married instead," Mom repeated to me.

I detected regret in many women of her generation. Some confided in me, "Life gets in the way. You'll see." No, I am going to fight. I thought about a plan. I could get married and quickly divorce. Then earn my college degree to show all these women the possibilities. I could be their inspiration. What a daydream. I could write a book about this. Or I could marry a man who supported me going to college and having a career. That would make a better inspirational book for girls and boys.

Mom and I drove Betsy to the heart of City Beautiful, University City's first name. "Who lives in these mansions?" Our house was tiny. I kept this thought to myself. It might anger her. Mom sometimes said I did not appreciate all of her and Dad's hard work to pay for our house. I loved our house. Mom would give my comment another meaning. Our street was named after a tree, not a university. When I have my own house, I will plant a hazelwood tree and a pear tree in my backyard to remind me of where I grew up.

Mom gave me a history lesson. "Famous architects built these mansions. Doctors, business owners, and lawyers to name a few lived here. These mansions were the first homes built in University City. Mansions were everywhere.

"I like the big house on Delmar with the large columns."

"You will be interested to hear that the resident of that mansion was a business partner of John C. Roberts, who lived in the mansion you love."

"Wow," was all I could say. I found it interesting that John C. Roberts preferred living in the country instead of with his associates and friends.

Mom continued, "People living here were probably antisemitic. There were no synagogues. They were in St. Louis City. Eventually, the only synagogue built was United Hebrew Temple on Skinner Boulevard across from Forest Park. It was built around 1920. Some nearby residents who owned these mansions sued to prevent the synagogue's construction. Litigation went all the way to the Missouri Supreme Court, which dismissed the lawsuit."

United Hebrew Temple is where all my cousins, aunts, and uncles on Dad's side of the family go to worship. It was Reform Judaism. The first time I went inside was to my Cousin Teddy's wedding. It was the most beautiful place. I wanted to go there, too.

"Too much like a church," I remember Dad saying. "They play the organ." On one of my library days, I looked this up. In 1818, an Austrian Talmudist, Eliezer Liebermann, wrote "The Bright Light," an article arguing that organ playing had been the Jewish custom in the Temple before the Christians adopted the instrument. I decided to keep this history to myself. Dad was raised Orthodox, so our choice was the middle path, Conservative. Mom stopped keeping a kosher house after Gary was born. Now, she cooks and serves pork chops, and Dad enjoys eating pork. I should read *Charlotte's Web* to my family.

I started thinking about what Mom told me. "Some places have a tavern on every corner. University City is graced with a synagogue on most corners." I reflected on the first synagogue and who owned the mansions. The first cultures of University City were French Catholics and Presbyterians. I read they believed in education. They sent their children to exclusive private schools such as John Burroughs, Country Day, and Mary Institute. Catholic girls went to Villa Duchesne, and boys went to St. Louis University High School, Chaminade, and other exclusive schools. Men were rich from professional careers. Some inherited wealth or married into wealth. Many successful men came from the South after the Civil War. Mom told me these men from the South started the Veiled Prophet Parade. Prior owners of my mansion were part of this culture. I wondered if they were antisemitic.

I remember Mom saying that some people who bought the mansions were doctors.

"Aren't all doctors Jewish?" I asked. Mom laughed.

"Only the doctors we see."

When we pulled into the parking lot at the University City Library, Dion was singing "Runaround Sue," a dancing song. Most songs talked about girls' broken hearts. This song told a tale about a girl who broke hearts. The song stayed playing in my head as I entered the library.

I returned a book and checked out another orange book while Mom waited in the car. It was easy to find a good book if I went directly to the orange books, the biographies.

I returned to the car with a book on the first Queen Elizabeth. Mom admired her. Both had red hair. Some called Queen Elizabeth, Bess. Mom talked about Queen Elizabeth as if she were a descendant of the Queen. Mom was excited I would read about Queen Elizabeth, and that made me happy.

"The Lion Sleeps Tonight" started to play on the radio as we drove home. "I Told Everyone" followed, and I sang along. Mom did not know this song. We pulled up in front of our house. Patsy Cline sang "Crazy." Mom knew this one.

Crazy, for thinking that my love could hold you
I'm crazy for trying and crazy for crying
And I'm crazy for loving you

We sang along, sitting in the car till the song was over. I hoped I never loved anyone who did not love me back. I told Mom, "I could be a singer like Judy Garland, my favorite."

"It is a sad life," she responded. "Best just to sing for pleasure, as birds do."

It takes 100 years for a memory to die unless continuously passed on to new generations. I decided to let Mom's unhappy childhood memories die with me. Best to honor the person she became.

Chapter 10:
Mrs. Frank's Vanity Dresser

We received real estate advertisements in the mail. I opened a flyer that showed Mrs. Frank's house at 7115 Willow Tree Lane for sale. This home was right behind my house. Our backyards were back-to-back. Dad told me the Franks probably bought this house for $12,000 in 1954. They were selling it for $15,000. I looked at the pictures of the remodeled home in the advertisement. Dad explained, "The real estate agent sends these out in hopes we will contact him to sell our house."

I will never forget Mrs. Frank planting flowers around the blue gazing ball in her backyard. She wore short shorts and a tube top, as did Mom when they gardened. Both women planted the same flowers: red, white, and purple petunias. However, my favorites were purple and yellow pansies. When the blue pansies came out, I begged Mom to buy those. "They did not seem as hardy," she concluded.

Beautiful, crystalized rocks bordered both gardens. I wondered if they would move the blue-mirrored gazing ball mounted on a concrete stand with them. I have heard it called a reflecting ball, too. I read gazing balls symbolize everything is going to be OK. I hope so.

Ricky Frank was my age. He went to my school, but we never had a class together. He had dark skin like his mother. I believe it is called an olive complexion. Very attractive. He looked like his mother with beautiful blond wavy hair, blue eyes, and a chiseled face. I loved his mother, Geraldine, or Gerry as we knew her.

Ricky was a crush. I pictured marrying Ricky and Mrs. Frank being my mother-in-law. Ricky and I would keep one or two of Vicky's puppies for our home. I do not remember having any interactions with Ricky. I do remember interactions with Mrs. Frank.

My long, blond, wavy hair tangled easily. Mom was not patient enough to get the knots out, and she pulled my hair, hurting me. I ran away from home once when Mom said it was time to wash my hair. "You have a sensitive scalp. Let's go to the beauty school on Delmar Boulevard once a week and get our hair done." She solved that problem for a while.

"Never cut your hair," Dad said. Good advice. Dad always complimented me. Later, I learned Dad saved a lock of my blonde hair after Mom trimmed it. It made me feel like a princess.

Mrs. Frank must have heard me screaming whenever Mom combed my hair. One day when I was swinging on my swing set, Mrs. Frank was in her backyard gardening and invited me into her house to detangle my hair. We went into her bedroom. There, she had a vanity table. Wow, I wanted one of those. Mrs. Frank told me, "Sit here, Linda, in my special vanity chair. It may not be comfortable. You can see yourself in the mirror."

I could also see Mrs. Frank's lipsticks and perfumes. She put some water on the ends of my hair. Mrs. Frank started at the bottom and painlessly worked the tangles out of my hair. She held the hair closer to my scalp while undoing the knots, and I did not feel pulling. I was going to try this method. I wanted to be independent of Mom combing my hair.

I returned home with beautifully combed hair. "I want a vanity dresser that matches Mrs. Frank's."

Mom replied, "You need a desk for a typewriter. I will buy a mirrored tray for the top of your dresser. I saw one at Sears. It was a mirror surrounded by gold-colored lacy metal. You can display perfume bottles, a handheld mirror, and jewelry. It will protect the white French provincial dresser top. We will go look at it." I started thinking about the desk and writing. She probably meant I needed a desk so I could learn to type fast and get a job as a secretary.

When she bought the mirrored tray and placed it on my white-and-gold French provincial dresser, I told Mom, "It is perfect. It reminds me of Mrs. Frank's vanity dresser." Then I looked over at my new desk, also French provincial. I was sure Louisa May Alcott had a desk, probably not a vanity dresser. The encyclopedia described her desk as very small. I read in one of those orange biography books Beatrix Potter changed rooms when she wrote. She had several small writing tables in various rooms. For a change, I wrote at the kitchen table. Other times, I wrote while sitting in my red rocking chair Uncle Louie, Mom's sister's husband, painted for me. Beatrix Potter self-published her first book, *The Tale of Peter Rabbit*. I will keep this information in mind.

Mrs. Frank was my friend. I liked having adults as friends. They were kind, centered on me, and helped me. I've mentioned that the Franks had a dog, Vicky. Vicky was the most beautiful white Spitz, an Eskimo dog. I wonder where they got such a beautiful dog. Vicky had puppies. I loved Vicky, and Mrs. Frank gave me a puppy. Vicky was the dog I told Mrs. McGee about and how I was too young to care for Vicky's puppy. I had to give the puppy back to Mrs. Frank.

The Franks moved from Willow Tree Lane in 1959. "We will have a swimming pool. Come over and swim," she told me. She knew I was sad. The invitation was not a substitute for having her within a fence climb. An older couple moved into the Frank's house. The husband told me to stay out of their backyard. I was stressed because Blackie sometimes climbed through the fence, and I had to retrieve him immediately. I could not waste time walking around the block. He could run off anywhere. I ran through their backyard anyway to find Blackie.

Gerald Frank, or Mr. Frank, built an expensive home further west, and Ricky went to a grade school in Ladue where rich people lived. Later in my detective work, reading old newspapers, I discovered Gerald and Geraldine met as students at Washington University in University City. Imagine when they met and found out they had the same first names. Jerry and Gerry. The opening to them dating and marrying. She was beautiful. Her father was a physician. Mr. Frank came from a working-class family. "He wanted to be rich," Mom said.

Mrs. Frank stayed in touch with Mom. She invited us to see the new home and swim in the backyard pool. Their new home was a classic ranch with a private, oversized lot and an in-ground swimming pool. I remember the pink brick on the home. I do not remember interacting with Ricky or his brother, Dicky, even though I did have a crush on Ricky at one time. I only remember being happy to see Mrs. Frank and Vicky again. The vanity dresser made the move to the new house. I was happy to see it. I wanted Mrs. Frank to invite me to sit on the vanity chair again so she could brush my hair, but she did not. I was afraid of Dicky. He killed my duck, Wacky. Mrs. Frank told me Dicky hugged it too hard. When I read *Of Mice and Men*, Dicky reminded me of Lennie Small because Lennie killed a pet mouse by hugging it too tightly. I still think Dicky strangled my pet duck out of meanness.

On the drive home, Mom asked, "How does a person go from a house like ours to that expensive house in five years? He sells used cars. I think Mr. Frank may get extra money. I heard he might be connected to mafia gambling and booking."

"I don't understand."

"Maybe Mr. Frank fixes bets on sports." I still needed to understand. "After all, he bought the house behind us in 1954 when he was in his twenties. Younger than most men in the subdivision."

"Maybe Mrs. Frank's dad gave them money to buy the house." I did not want to think Mrs. Frank was involved with a dishonest person.

"Hmmm, you could be right. Mrs. Frank's father is a doctor and could have given them the down payment."

"What about the pink brick?" I asked.

"No, and the white carpet is not my style."

We never saw her again. They lived in the pink brick house for just a few years, then bought a house in California in 1963. Mom heard they bought a mansion on a cliff. She expanded her family with another son and, thankfully, a daughter. She needed a daughter. I thought about Mrs. Frank off and on. Did she think of me?

Tragedy hit. Mom came into my room and looked sad.

"What's wrong?" I asked.

"Mrs. Frank is dead."

"No. What? How? She is so young."

"Her car went off a cliff. It was a brand-new Thunderbird. Her new Thunderbird rolled from their driveway through a twelve-foot retaining wall and over a seventy-foot cliff. She was found dead, barefoot, and in her housecoat."

Now I was scared. Why would Mrs. Frank be driving in her housecoat and barefoot? The detective in me assumed she was dead, and then someone placed Mrs. Frank in the car. Somebody made the car with her body in it go off the cliff.

Mom continued. "There is a movie called *Angel Face*. It reminds me of this." Mom started to tell me the story. "Jean Simmons plays the main character. Her name is Diane. One afternoon, as Diane's father and stepmother start their car to drive to town, their vehicle mysteriously reverses. It careens backward down a cliff, killing both occupants. As Diane is the sole heir to their fortune, she comes under suspicion for murder. Suspicion is also cast on Frank, played by Robert Mitchum, her boyfriend/husband, for possibly tampering with the vehicle. The trial ends in acquittal. However, Frank immediately tells Diane he is ending their sham marriage.

Consequently, Diane's mental condition deteriorates, and her sense of guilt leads her to confess to Frank she was responsible for the mechanical manipulation that caused the death of her parents. Frank makes one last trip to the estate to gather his belongings. He then waits for a taxi to take him to a bus station, but Diane offers a ride instead. He gets into her car. After putting the car in gear, Diane accelerates backward, crashing down the cliff. Frank and Diane die."

"Did someone kill Mrs. Frank? Did the idea come from that movie?" I started to think about the main character's name, Frank. Frank and Frank.

"I think it may be the mafia. Remember, I said Mr. Frank may have been involved in illegal betting. Mr. Frank did not want an investigation. He may have been afraid for his safety and the safety of his children, or he may have done something connected to her murder."

"Was it a suicide? The Mrs. Frank I knew was not suicidal. Did she become suicidal?"

"No, no, no," Mom declared. "We do not know what caused her death. Maybe it was an accident." We wanted it to be an accident.

Then Mom said, "Some husbands want to get rid of their wives. A husband might kill his wife, so he does not have to pay alimony. The death looks like an accident."

Did Mrs. Frank die because her husband wanted an expensive lifestyle? I believed she was happy wearing short shorts and a tube top, planting annuals around a blue reflecting ball. When she finished, she would go inside her house to comb her daughter's curly hair and stop to pet her dog, Vicky.

Chapter 11:
Work, Create, Build Gifts from Bubbe

In a few months, I will be nine years old. I am in third grade with my favorite teacher, Miss Ackerman. She likes me, too. Mom and I invited her to our home for lunch one day. Mom cooked Campbell's Tomato Soup and grilled-cheese sandwiches. I hope she did not mind eating vegetarian. She invited us to her wedding. I had to borrow a dress to wear. I did not have anything fancy. The dress I borrowed was peach lace with a satin sash. The dress was pretty, but not the color. Many people attended. She married James Stuart Bowie, a descendant of the Bowie who invented the famous Bowie knife. I was excited because I thought he was a cowboy. Not so. When she became pregnant, we brought a baby present to her apartment. It was a large apartment building on Meramec Avenue before North and South Boulevard. I envisioned myself her age living there. This apartment was close to all my favorite places—Velvet Freeze, the hobby shop, and Famous-Barr Department Store.

One day she announced the class was going to play a vocabulary game. We were assigned a partner. The words chosen were from the back pages of our reading book. Steve Stein was my assigned partner. He was smart. Steve sat on the edge of his desk chair all day. When he knew the answer, he waved his arm excitedly. I thought he would fall out of his seat. Every night I studied the vocabulary words and memorized their meanings. We missed winning by one team. Steve blamed me for losing and became combustible. I could see him becoming a lawyer. It probably was my fault. I studied less the evening before the last competition. I had a lot going on at home.

First, Mom was stressed. Then Dad was stressed. He was studying for his real estate license. The family thought being a real estate agent fit him. He loved to talk to people. He would enjoy driving people around in his car and showing properties. Dad rode the train to Jefferson City, Missouri, to take his real estate exam. He had to hurry back home because his mom died, my Bubbe.

I only had my grandmother, Bubbe, for a short time. Yet, she is the most important person in my life. Even though I was eight when she died, she gave me everything I appreciate about myself and the world. Everyone in the family loved her. She was the only person I knew that had this status. No one argued with her or told her what to do. No one said an unkind word against her. Even Mom adored her. Her name was Hilda Kramer Fine. She and her husband, my grandfather, Joseph Fine, were in love as young people. In Lithuania, Jewish marriages were arranged. Dad told me this story.

"Hilda, your Bubbe stood up to her parents and the matchmaker. She told them she was marrying Joseph Fine." From that story, I got my self-confidence. My trust in myself. What a cute couple. They were both no more than five feet three inches tall. Joseph was a blacksmith in the old country. In America, he became a cobbler, mending shoes and boots. Hilda was a fine cook and baker. She was the brains of the family.

I called her Bubbe, pronounced with short u and e. It means "grandmother" in Yiddish. She was beautiful. She had a pug nose. Bubba wore her silver hair in a bun. I never knew the length of her hair. Was her hair wavy like mine? Everyone who knew the two of us told me I resembled her. When I heard this, I felt proud. I liked myself more and more because of Bubbe. I felt beautiful knowing people believed I favored her. I embraced aging when just a child. I couldn't wait to look like Bubbe. Here is an example of my defense of older people.

I was standing in a park. It was winter and an extra-cold day. I wore a long coat. I wrapped my head and neck in a long scarf I had knitted. I crossed my arms around each other for extra warmth. My shoulders were reaching for my ears.

"You remind me of an old woman," a friend told me. He meant it as an insult. I took it as a compliment. We were not friends afterward.

Dad had a routine with Bubbe. After work on Friday, he picked up homemade challah and kamish bread cookies from Bubbe and brought them home to me. I ate the goodies with a cup of hot Lipton tea. On Sundays, Dad drove me over to her apartment to visit. When Grandpa, Zayde, was still alive, he sat in the living room smoking a waterpipe. Dad explained, "It helps with his asthma." I wondered if I would have to smoke a waterpipe when I got old because I, too, had asthma.

"Why doesn't Zayde talk to us?" I asked.

"During the Depression, he lost his shoe cobbler business. He stopped speaking English. He only speaks Yiddish now." I should say something to him. I never did. He died when I was about six years old from congestive heart failure.

I saw Bubbe more when Zayde died. She babysat at our house when Mom and Dad had an evening out. Bubbe had a strong Yiddish accent. I listened carefully to make out each word. Later, this helped me understand other people who spoke with foreign accents. That was one gift she gave me.

Bubbe gave me irreplaceable gifts. Not all of them are material. One Sunday afternoon, she took me outside to her apartment backyard. We had to climb down a twisty iron staircase. When we reached the tiny patch of grass, she handed me a bag filled with bread. "Tear off small pieces and throw them on the ground." I did. Suddenly, a flock of pigeons appeared on the wires. "Stand very still." I did. The pigeons quickly approached me, looking for bread and eating pieces. They surrounded my feet. I experienced my first wild bird encounter. Birds connected me to nature. Bubba gave me the gift of loving birds. I started feeding the birds in my backyard. Uncle Freddie, Mom's brother, gave me my first parakeet when I was maybe six. I have never been without a pet bird since.

Almost every time Bubbe and I got together, she gave me a handkerchief she crocheted around the edges. The handkerchiefs crocheted in periwinkle blue were my favorite. I never used them. I could not imagine getting them dirty with boogers and snot. I cherished the handkerchiefs until Mom or someone cleaned out the drawer, and they were gone. I learned to take better care of precious items, a lesson Bubbe taught me.

The most significant gift she gave me was my love of Judaism and old-world culture. Every year, Dad's family got together for Hanukkah and Passover. Bubbe and Zayde hosted. There were a lot of us. Eight adults and ten children. There would be more children later. Tables lined up from the dining room through the living room to the bay window sitting area. As families grew, we no longer shared holidays with Dad's family. I missed these gatherings. Mom's family did not know how to perform the Passover seder and they did not celebrate Hanukkah.

One old-world tradition was pinching children's cheeks and calling them "Punum." It was a compliment. It meant the child was adorable. Uncle Abe, Dad's older brother, had this tradition of pinching my cheek and pinching hard. It left a red mark. I dreaded seeing him because of this tradition. One evening, he was about to pinch my cheek, and I yelled, "No, you hurt me." I ran over to Mom. Everyone turned to look at me and then at him. He never pinched my cheek again. I felt brave sticking up for myself. I was about four years old. I felt terrible because Abe was Dad's protector growing up. Dad had to understand. Enough is enough. After all, Bubbe taught me to be brave.

Being Jewish and being brave go together. Bubbe saw parts of her village in Lithuania destroyed by Russians mandated by the czar. The czar hated Jews. "Why do people hate and kill Jews," I asked Mom.

"As a people, we are kicked out of different countries for being successful. Did you know some Christians believe Jews have horns?" We laughed. I started thinking about how groups of people prefer to be with people who have traits in common. Catholics have their schools. Wealthy people prefer to join country clubs with people of the same status, political beliefs, and religion. People build hospitals for specific religions. We are different tribes. I thought about Indians. They do not mix. Each tribe sticks together. They too, fight amongst the various tribes. Yet, my best friend is not Jewish. The boys I am attracted to are not Jewish. I sat silently, thinking about how I loved my Jewish culture and still gravitated toward non-Jews.

Then Mom said, "Maybe people from different ethnicities should mix more. When we stay separated, we do not understand each other." I would remember this comment.

"Who are famous Jews?" I asked Mom.

"Jesus may be the most famous Jew! Some Christians hate us because we do not believe Jesus is the Messiah. He was a great Jew."

"If he was Jewish, why do some Christians hate Jews? Why do some Christians kill people if they believe in Jesus?"

Mom replied, "Maybe some Christians do not know Jesus was Jewish. They blame his death on Jews. But then some preach Jesus' death was God's plan. I am confused by all this. Christians try to convert people to their religion. Jews do not. When you are older, read the history of the Crusades. Catholics tortured and killed Jews in Rome, Spain, and England, trying to convert Jews. Jews who discovered God! The Church did the same in this country and in Canada to Indians. They punished or killed non-believers. Would Jesus support that? Jews were forbidden to own land during the Middle Ages. Later, they could not buy houses, only rent. Jews were denied participation in some careers, even in this country. Some universities do not allow Jews to attend."

We sat in silence. I did not understand how people could kill in the name of God to try to convert people to a religion. Wasn't religion supposed to be for peace?

Mom continued, "In the past, Christians have taken away land, heritage, and language from people who do not believe in Jesus. Missionaries became a way to make a living. They promoted Christianity in foreign countries sometimes killing or punishing natives who refused to convert.

After a while, Mom added, "People derive a sense of superiority for themselves because of their faith."

When conversations became too scary or serious, Mom had a way of moving on. "Back to famous Jews. There is Albert Einstein."

"What did he do?" I asked.

"I do not understand it. Einstein had a role in the science behind the atomic bomb. The bomb ended World War II. Most of the scientists who created the atomic bomb were Jewish."

"Who else is famous?" I asked.

"Jonas Salk created the polio vaccine," she smiled.

"I remember the shot."

"Marc Chagall is a famous artist. I will show you his paintings in the art books downstairs. Almost all the famous movie stars and comedians are Jewish. Paul Newman is Jewish."

"He is handsome. I think Cousin David has those same blue eyes."

"Here is a surprise. Did you know the famous words on the Statue of Liberty were taken from a poem by Emma Lazarus, who was Jewish?"

"You mean, 'Give me your tired, your poor, your huddled masses yearning to breathe free'?"

"I am impressed you know that. Ironically, the United States only allowed a few Jews into our country when Hitler was murdering them."

Mom taught me more, "Then there are famous musicians. Jewish composers wrote the most popular Christmas songs." Mom listed these songs: "Silver Bells", "White Christmas", and "Rudolph the Red-Nosed Reindeer". We sang all these songs at school. Steve Stein protested. He told the Jewish kids in class not to sing these songs. I sang them anyway. We needed to acknowledge that we were not the only culture, just the majority.

"I believe Jews have won the most Nobel Prizes, given our population's size. Many authors are Jewish," Mom added.

I blurted out, "Was Louisa May Alcott Jewish?" I crossed my fingers.

"She did not practice Judaism. She did have Jewish ancestry. Her mother's grandfather, Joseph May, was a descendant of Portuguese Jews. Louisa May Alcott practiced Unitarianism, but the family, I read, took pride in Jewish ancestry. May is a famous name in St. Louis. They had a department store downtown. They were Jewish. May is a Jewish name."

I was stunned. I was going to ask about Unitarianism, but I forgot. My favorite writer was Jewish! I sat in silence, thinking about this new information. I had many things in common with my favorite writer. I was happy. Did she love birds?

Mom added, "Some Jews converted to other Christian religions so they would not be killed. It's best to choose life. Many practiced their Judaism in secret."

I felt empowered by Mom's list of famous Jewish people. I thought about my family history. Zayde and my Dad's older sister Bess left Bubbe, Abe, and Dad to go to America. Zayde only had the money for him and Aunt Bess to leave Lithuania. The plan was to get to America, make money, and send money back to Bubbe. Then she and the boys would join Zayde and Bess. Abe was about twelve years old. Dad was about five years old. They started their long journey to Japan, led by Bubbe. They stayed with a Jewish family in Japan until more money arrived. From

Japan, they went to the West Coast of America, then took a train to St. Louis, Missouri. Dad enjoyed telling this story. "At the beginning of our travels, we were in a wagon pulled by horses. We were going to the train station. A hoodlum jumped up on the wagon and stole a suitcase. Abe jumped off the wagon and ran after the hoodlum. The hoodlum dropped the suitcase." Dad respected Abe.

Dad called Abe for advice later in life. Mom said. "We don't need his advice." Mom did not understand how Abe protected Dad when Dad was a boy. She did not understand many things about Dad's upbringing. Mom only experienced Dad's adult siblings meddling in her life. It seemed to cause a barrier between families.

Talking to Mom and Dad, I learned Jews fought off the labeling of victimhood. "Whatever they do to us, we will work, create, and build" was repeatedly voiced in family chats.

My 78-year-old Bubbe was not a victim. She was brave. She died because she tried climbing into her apartment window after she locked herself out. The window was open, and independent Hilda thought she could climb through the opening. She fell, broke her hip, and never recovered. When Bubbe died, Dad was in Jefferson City taking his real estate license exam. He took the train home, and we met him at Union Station.

I should have comforted Dad more. We lost our favorite person. This taught me to cherish old people. Keep them close. Listen to their stories. Learn to bake their recipes. Grandparents are not with us for long. Talk about grandparents to the next generation to keep grandparents alive. Most important, children need extra attention when they lose a loved one. I threw a tantrum because no one acknowledged I lost my Bubbe.

Chapter 12:
Gentile Side of the Neighborhood

Mrs. Daniels was our crosswalk guard. She assisted whenever a child needed to cross Partridge Avenue during school hours. We felt safe seeing her. I lived on the same side of the street as the school, a block away. I only needed her assistance if I visited a friend who lived on the east side of Partridge Avenue. I always waved to Mrs. Daniels when she was not helping children cross the street. Partridge Avenue was a street people took from Page Boulevard to Olive Street Road and vice versa. Partridge Avenue could get traffic but only a little.

Sometimes, for variety, I walked halfway down Hazelwood Lane to the walkway built between houses. It landed me at the playground behind the school. The developer of our subdivision, Sam Ladd, must have had children and thought a walkway through the subdivision to the school would be a good idea, staying off the busier street, Partridge Avenue. It was a good idea. Jimmy Reina's house was on one side of the walkway. They had a beautiful patio and yard. I walked by, hoping Mrs. Reina would be outside. We always talked. She was Hollywood beautiful. Mrs. Reina was the only mom I knew who had long hair. Before Ray Daniels, I had a crush on Jimmy Reina. When I was four years old, I came home one day crying.

"Mom, Mom," I sobbed. "I can't marry Jimmy Reina because he's not Jewish."

"Who said that?"

"Don't Jewish people only marry Jewish people?"

"No, not always," Mom told me. "Sometimes, love is more important than rules." I could not believe what she was saying. It was the beginning of crushes on boys who were not Jewish, Gentiles. Mom must have been in love with a Gentile at one time. I started to think I was going to marry a Gentile. One who got me and was not going ask me to change my culture for him.

Everyone walked to school and home unless they had to go somewhere else. Then their parents picked them up. Many of us went home for lunch. That is why Mrs. Daniels' job as the crosswalk guard was so important. We felt protected by her, and she was a mom. She was the mom of Ray and Sue, friends to everyone. Mrs. Daniels became the mom of all of us. Mrs. Daniels sat in her car on cold days, waiting for children to show up needing her assistance. She used a hand-held STOP sign. She knew all our names. Mrs. Daniels was always the first person in the street and the last person out of the street.

Wherever I walked, I turned around periodically to make sure no one was following me. That's because Mom told me scary stories over and over and over about girls getting kidnapped. I felt Mrs. Daniels would hear me scream and come to my rescue. She was tall and strong. She had access to the police phone on Partridge Avenue.

I mentioned she had a son named Ray and a daughter named Sue. Ray was in my grade, and Sue was a year older. Ray and I had many classes together. Ray was athletic, smart, and kind. In sixth grade, we had dance lessons in gym class on Fridays. My favorite time was when Ray was my dance partner. I remember a school trip to the St. Louis Art Museum. Ray and I sat together on the bus. Heaven. When Ray and I entered the museum, I felt embarrassed seeing all the naked statues in the museum's lobby. I had been in this lobby many times and never felt uncomfortable.

We had a writing assignment for school. We had to interview someone and write up the interview. I decided to interview Mrs. Daniels. I pretended I was a reporter. I called her on the telephone.

While talking with her, I realized the Roberts (second and third generations) still lived in the mansion when she moved to the neighborhood. She remembers the fields before they became University Forest Elementary School. She never explored the Roberts' land. It was private property, she said. She did remember seeing the old wooden farmhouse from Partridge Avenue.

"Private property did not stop me," I said. We laughed. "I explored the Roberts' property bought by the Central Seventh-Day Adventist Church, which established the St. Louis Junior Academy parochial school. I became friends with Mrs. McGee, the cook, her sons, and her dog. Mrs. McGee gave me a puppy, my dog, Blackie." I elaborated on how the cook explained that I could no longer visit the private property. "They said I was trespassing."

Mrs. Daniels said, "Sue and Ray explored the property owned by the orphanage across the street from our house. The nuns warned them to stay off the orphanage property. Both properties were tempting to kids who sought out nature and wanted to explore. The orphanage had unusual trees. There were ornamental trees from different countries. Who can forget the persimmon and buckeye trees on the orphanage property?"

"The ginkgo tree was my favorite," I told her. "It turned a bright yellow in the fall." I kept bringing up the mansion. "The mansion has those Osage orange trees that produce big bumpy fruits like grapefruits. We played catch with them. The cook's sons, who live there, told me they placed the fruits on Partridge Avenue and waited for cars to run them over, making a big splash. I fretted an Osage orange would fall from the tree on my head. I never saw these trees anywhere else. I looked them up in my encyclopedia. They grow in the South." Then a thought came. Maybe I should study trees and write about trees. My thoughts started to wander.

Mrs. Daniels changed the topic back to the orphanage, "I met one of the orphans. He told me there was a tornado before we moved in on Raymond Avenue. One of the Roberts' oak trees in front of the mansion fell. A huge honeybee hive was exposed. Mrs. Roberts collected the honey and took it to the orphanage for the children to enjoy. I also heard Mrs. Roberts delivered milk and eggs to the neighbors during World War II".

"I wish I could have met all the people who lived in the mansion." Then I brought the conversation back to Mrs. Daniels. After all, I was supposed to be interviewing her and not gathering information about the mansion. "I feel safe seeing you outside the school every day." I could sense she was smiling.

"I found a letter you wrote to Ray in school last year. I gave it to him recently," she confided. I was surprised.

"We learned how to write letters in class. We wrote different types of letters to each other. I must have written Ray a letter to a friend, not a business letter." She did not offer any information about the letter. I was disappointed.

I learned when a conversation starts to end, a person will say what is most important. Our conversation turned to education and the many benefits of living in our neighborhood. Mrs. Daniels' voice became more serious.

"People here have their churches and synagogues they support. In addition, they support public education. We all vote for higher taxes to keep the schools in excellent condition. Teachers receive a good salary. They stay working here. We get the best teachers. The playground has a variety of equipment for all the children. Different size pullup bars for little kids and big kids. Softball and soccer fields for the athletes. Hopscotch and square ball courts for others." That's me, I thought. "The school offers music and art classes. Teachers take students on field trips to see historical places. They learn about careers by visiting the water plant and where the newspaper is published. Guest speakers present additional expertise to students."

I told her about the man who came to our class and explained water conservation a few years ago. I did not tell her his talk made me forever anxious when I now see or hear water wasted. She said, "Ray was excited to learn about the space program because the teacher had the space launches on the TV. Hands-on education, not just telling students information. They experience the information."

She talked about the development of being a good citizen. "Parents are involved in the school." My mom was involved though I noticed her involvement was less when she started working. I asked Mrs. Daniels if there was anything else she wanted me to add to my report.

"Only that I love living here and raising my children in this special place." Like a good reporter, I thanked Mrs. Daniels for her time.

I valued talking with Mrs. Daniels, asking her questions, and getting interesting information. I read through my notes to decide the content of my report. Using quotes was new. I changed a few words in some of Mrs. Daniels' quotes for readability. After dinner, Mom helped me add the quotation marks to the report. The quotes gave life to the assignment. I typed up the assignment. It took forever because I did not know how to type like a real typist. I needed a secretary. I understood the value of secretaries. I still did not want to be one. After I typed my report, I wished I had asked Mrs. Daniels if she named Ray after the street, Raymond Avenue, where they lived. Reporters always wish they had asked more questions.

Here is my report. I kept it short to meet the assignment requirements. I learned much more.

Mrs. Daniels

The family moved to Raymond Avenue in 1951. The house was brand-new. Mrs. Daniels was a practicing Catholic, and the family attended church on Sundays. Mr. Daniels was not religious. They talked about sending their children to Catholic schools. However, Mr. Daniels wanted his children to have a broader education and attend public schools. University Forest Elementary School was that place where education was valued. The school had an active Parent Teacher Association. That involvement contributed to the school's high rating. She reported, "Just as if going to a private prep school. For non-Jewish children attending University Forest Elementary School, it was an opportunity to learn about the Jewish traditions."

Mrs. Daniels ended our conversation by telling me, "University City may not have the greatest football team, but it does have many Merit Scholarship recipients. In Missouri, it has a 10 rating, the highest. I enjoy my job as a school crosswalk guard. I know everyone. My children love this special place. Maybe my grandchildren will live here, too."

A year later, the *St. Louis Post Dispatch* newspaper published an article about crosswalk guards working in various areas of St. Louis County. Mrs. Daniels was featured. There was a picture of her standing in the middle of Partridge Avenue, holding up a STOP sign while children crossed the street. I showed the newspaper to Mom and Dad. Mom noted, "I remember the interview you did with Mrs. Daniels, and I helped you with the quotation marks for your report."

Dad added, "You are ahead of the news."

Chapter 13:
A Day at the Library

It was Christmas break. Dad poured another cup of coffee. I walked outside to check on Blackie. I brought Blackie a soup bone to chew so he would have something to do all day. Mom left for work.

Mom works at Stix, Baer, and Fuller Department Store. Today, Mom was working all day. She sells notions. Notions are odds and ends that do not fit elsewhere in the store. Mom sold scarves, handkerchiefs, wallets, fancy writing pens, sewing materials, greeting cards, stationery, and more. Mom also worked part-time collecting marketing research in our neighborhood on various new products, such as instant mashed potatoes. I liked this job because she took me with her. She told me when she knocked on a door with me by her side, people were more friendly.

Gary rode his bike over to Fred's house. He was thirteen years old and independent. I packed a peanut butter and grape jelly sandwich and a lunch-size bag of Fritos in my plaid lunch box with a matching thermos filled with Kool-Aid. I did not drink milk unless it was chocolate. Dad gave me two quarters in case I needed anything else. I always carried a dime to make a phone call. On the drive to the library, I started thinking about the bakery on Delmar. I might stroll the aisles of the dime store, Kresge's, or Woolworths. I can't remember which one. Dad pulled his car into the University City Library parking lot. I arrived at about 10:00 am.

"I will pick you up at 4:00 pm." Long day at the library, I thought. "Do not leave the library," Dad repeated.

I descended the metal steps to the side door of the library. I always used this door instead of the main entrance. I looked around for an empty table. I placed my lunch box on the tabletop and my red wool coat over a chair. I wanted to take up as much room as possible so no one could sit at my table. I looked around. It's going to be a long day. I'll look at the orange books first. I first spotted *The Odyssey of Homer*. I did not know what those words meant. Someday I would. I scanned more books. There was *Abraham Lincoln: The Prairie Years*, *John Quincy Adams: Boy Patriot*, and *The Life of Daniel Boone*. *Newspaper Days 1899-1906* caught my attention. I want to write for a newspaper. My class at school took a bus trip downtown to see how the *St. Louis Post-Dispatch* was printed. My Uncle Freddy worked as a printer. I took the book to the librarian.

"Interested in journalism?" She could see I was not familiar with the word. She clarified, "It means writing for a newspaper?"

"I want to be a writer. Louisa May Alcott is my favorite writer. I want to write about my childhood."

"Are you here by yourself?"

I nodded yes. "My name is Linda Fine. I live on Hazelwood Lane off Partridge."

"What a coincidence. You live near the Roberts' mansion. He owned a newspaper, *The St. Louis Star and Times*."

"My mom told me he owned a shoe company."

"That too. Mr. Roberts was an important person in St. Louis. Do you want to see some of the newspapers he published?"

"Yes." I explained to her I loved the mansion. It was my favorite place. I even thought of it as my mansion. I told her about the people who live there now and the private Adventist school. I told her about Blackie, my dog, and how the school's cook gave me Blackie from her dog's litter of puppies.

"I can help you find information about your mansion and its history."

I lit up with excitement. The day was not going to be boring. What a coincidence, I wanted to work for a newspaper, and the mansion owner owned a newspaper.

"Need paper to take notes?" I nodded yes. She disappeared and returned with a yellow pad of lined paper and a few newspapers for me to read.

"Thank you so much. May I borrow a pencil?" She smiled and gave me a pencil.

She took my library card and checked out my book. I now had the book on the history of newspapers for two weeks. She handed me back my library card, and I thanked her again. Before I left the library check-out area, she told me some history.

"A business partner of John C. Roberts built this whole area. His name was Edward Gardner Lewis. Lewis was the first mayor of University City. He was a publisher, too. Roberts and Lewis owned the same newspaper at one time. Lewis built the Lions Gate. The current City Hall was his business location. He built his mansion, which later burned down in Lewis Park, where the mansions surround a lake. He named it after himself. He was responsible for all those mansions around Lewis Park." *Where the Presbyterians live*, I thought to myself. I wondered if she was Presbyterian. She did not look Jewish.

"My brother and I fish at Lewis Park. Rich people live around the lake. Lawyers."

She smiled. "Lewis created University City and the 1904 World's Fair." I now knew I wanted to study to be a newspaper writer. I learned the word journalism. I could be a journalist and also write books. I could buy one of the homes around Lewis Park if the Presbyterians did not protest. I remembered the story Mom told me about the people living in Lewis Park not wanting a Jewish synagogue near them. I'd show them that living well is the best revenge when I move into Lewis Park. I will be a famous writer, and they will want my autograph.

I returned to my table. Relieved no one was there. I spread out the newspapers. I took up the whole table legitimately. Later, the librarian brought me more newspaper articles, including information about Roberts' death. I could not believe I was reading newspapers printed by the man who lived in the mansion about the man who lived in the mansion. He died in 1924. His sons Elzey Meacham Roberts and John C. Roberts, Jr., took over the newspaper. The newspaper went out of business the year I was born, 1951. The sons got into the radio business, KXOK. John C. Roberts' wife, Anna, died in 1954. Elzey Meacham Roberts sold everything that year and bought a house on an exclusive golf course. He sold the mansion's land to Sam Ladd. Ladd sold the mansion to the Seventh-Day Adventist Church with about four acres.

A picture of my mansion in the newspaper explained all of this. I got the chills. Elzey Meacham Roberts turned KXOK, the radio station, over to his son, Elzey Meacham Roberts, Jr. Elzey Meacham Roberts, Jr. sold the radio station for 1.5 million dollars in 1960. My head was spinning with all this information. I needed to move. I told the librarian I was going outside for a few minutes. If I were older, I would have smoked a cigarette like professional reporters and writers do. I walked back and forth because I told Dad I would not leave the library. While I was pacing, I wondered if Roberts had built my mansion. Everyone assumed he did. I approached the librarian and asked her how I could find out.

"You're sounding like an investigative reporter." I smiled. She showed me how to research for my answer. Here is what I found.

Eugene Hunt Benoist built the home at 1433 Partridge Avenue in the 1880s. He owned several lots south of the mansion. They were fields previously owned by the Anselms. The Anselms were farmers. There once was a two-story frame farmhouse about where my school is now located. This farmhouse keeps popping up in conversations. Benoist was in the real-estate business. He named the area Benoist Heights. He wanted to subdivide the land into numerous small lots. Fortunately, the fields remained until my subdivision was built in 1954.

I found a horrific story. Benoist had a daughter my age, ten. Her name was Elmira Clemence Benoist, 1886-1896. The newspaper heading announced, "Child's Awful Fate." The article read:

She was an expert pony rider. Her uncle gave her a polo pony after she admired the pony. She was passionate about riding. A familiar sight in her neighborhood. I pictured her riding all through my neighborhood when it was fields and orchards.

Out for her usual afternoon canter, she left her home on Partridge Avenue for Page Avenue riding westward all the way to Hanley Road.

The conductor, James Walton, noted her presence. He was familiar with her riding alongside the train. Cantering ahead of the train. When the train turned around at the end of the track near Hanley Road, she was ahead at a good pace. When Partridge Avenue was approaching, he expected her to turn in front of the train to go home so he slowed down. But she kept riding straight down Page Avenue going east. The conductor then increased his speed, thinking she was riding alongside the train. The golden curls of Elmira floating in the breeze while riding were admired by the passengers. They watched with keen pleasure. Passengers commented on the rare beauty of the child riding the horse. They heard her merry laugh as she gained upon the train. She won the hearts of all on board. They hoped she would win the race. Believing she had accomplished her goal of defeating the train, she waved her hat to the passengers right at the corner of her street, Partridge Avenue. Just as she saluted her victory, the pony made the jump that unseated her. She uttered a shriek, heard by her mother. Suddenly, 30 feet past Partridge the pony became unmanageable, turned right, and leaped across the railroad tracks, directly in front of the train.

I thought about my own experiences on a horse. When a horse gets close to the barn, it increases its speed. There is no stopping or turning around. I assumed the pony was hungry or tired. It was late afternoon about 4:30.

The sudden swirling around and leaping of the pony caused Elmira to fall onto the tracks. Onto the tracks in front of the train.

The conductor applied the brakes full force when he saw the pony turn and leap across the tracks but could not stop to avoid Elmira lying on the tracks. The train stopped 20 feet after it crushed the life out of Elmira.

When the wheels had done their deadly work, no one had the courage to go to the scene. Elmira was under the car. Her blond curls admired the moment before were now matted with blood. The lady passengers fainted; the men sickened. Her mother ran to the scene. The child was taken from her mother's arms and brought to the mansion. Her funeral service was held at the mansion. All her classmates attended.

I wondered what had happened to the pony.

I never knew my mansion had a history. Elmira reminded me of my best friend, Janice. She loved horses, was spirited, and dreamt of owning a horse.

I started daydreaming. Maybe University City would buy my mansion from the Adventist Church. My mansion could be a registered historic building used for events such as weddings and graduations. I see it as a science center for grade school kids. Classrooms of children could walk two blocks to the mansion. They would find bugs, learn about butterflies, identify trees, and listen to bird songs. They could debate if my three-legged turtle was born with only three legs or did it lose a limb in an accident or fight. The turtle could be inspirational because it lived successfully with only three legs. The turtle would be an introduction to people with disabilities. A groundskeeper would make sure the arbor blossomed with award-winning roses. I imagined the reflecting pond repaired by a community donor. When rented out for parties, guests checked in at the gazebo.

Parents could rent the mansion for Bar Mitzvah parties. I wanted to be married there. I saw myself posing for pictures with the blue morning glories in the background. My parents would live at 7114 Hazelwood Lane into their old age.

I imagined visiting the neighborhood with my own family. I envisioned my daughter and I walking the grounds of the mansion. "Don't pick any of the flowers," I'd tell her, remembering my rogue past. Lots of stories to tell. "Blackie was born here." She would then say she wanted a puppy. I would tell my daughter, "Caring for a dog is a responsibility." Even mansions have what-ifs.

I returned to investigating facts. I then learned Max R. Orthwein bought the mansion in 1900. Orthwein named it Orthwein Heights. The carriage house was added to the mansion in 1900 by the new owner, who loved horses and carriage racing. Orthwein built a carriage racing track around the property. He hosted extravagant outdoor parties with lights and lanterns strung around the front-yard arbor and gardens. Here is a description of one party I found published in June 1902 in the *St. Louis Post-Dispatch*.

Nowhere was there a greater air of festivities than at Orthwein Heights, the beautiful country home of Mr. Orthwein. The spacious house, surrounded by the velvety lawn, was decked with greens and flowers. The lawn was transformed into a fairyland by the lavish use of hundreds of colored electric lights, which were festooned from trees and shrubs. Erected on the side lawn was a gaily colored tent. This sheltered a long board of plenty where lemonade, punch, and supper were served buffet. There were outdoor amusements for their guests. Well's Band played during the entire evening.

I could visualize the parties at the mansion. It was designed for parties. Orthwein lived there till 1905. The Orthwein family moved to Kansas City. He was in a car accident. I read the descendants gave much to the St. Louis community in charity and volunteer activities. Their love of horses was passed on to later generations.

Next came the Roberts family. I found three generations of Roberts. John C. Roberts bought the mansion in 1905. He was more creative and named his newly bought country estate, Crest Haven. It was going to be his forever home. He created a family crest and hung it near the mansion's carved walnut staircase.

I drew a family tree of the Roberts family. It helped organize decedents who lived in the mansion.

Particular Place and People

```
John C. Roberts          Anna Kaiser
  1853–1924               Roberts
                         1866-1954


John C. Roberts Jr.   Elzey Meacham    Isabella Wells
   1897–1965             Roberts          Roberts
                        1892–1962        1895–1984


                      Elzey Meacham    Isabella Roberts
                       Roberts, Jr.      1934-present
                       1920 – 2010
```

I was starving. I asked the librarian, "Is it OK for me to eat my sandwich at the table?"

"Eat in our lunchroom," she insisted as she led me to a room that had a few tables. This room had windows. I sat at the small table next to the window. I thanked the librarian. She came back with her lunch. We ate together.

"How old are you?" she asked.

"I am ten."

"I thought you might be younger."

"Everyone thinks that." It was the vegetarian diet. It kept me thin and short.

"You will appreciate looking young someday." She did not know I wanted to be old. "Tell me about the Roberts' place." Where to begin? No one ever asked me to talk about my favorite place.

Later, I used the two quarters my dad gave me to copy newspaper articles. I had never used a copy machine before. The librarian showed me how. I had the best day. I thanked the librarian over and over.

I was starving again and couldn't wait to get home. One thing I learned about being a vegetarian is I am always hungry. I walked outside and looked for Dad's car.

"How was your day?" he asked as I settled into the car with my papers, book, and lunchbox.

"Great! I learned newspapers are an easy way to find information. I am going to be a journalist and a writer." Dad never told me to be a secretary. "I met the nicest librarian. I want to go back soon. I spent the quarters you gave me on copying articles from newspapers."

He could see the yellow paper pad with papers hanging out the sides. I told him what I learned. Dad told me, "I stocked and sold shoes made by International Shoe Company, the company Roberts owned when I was a teenager." He never met Roberts. Roberts died in 1924 when Dad was about fourteen years old. I was impressed by John C. Roberts. I believed Dad was impressive for supporting his family as a teenager. I wish I had told him.

"Imagine owning a newspaper and the largest shoe manufacturing company, too," I excitedly told Dad. Everything is connected. We stopped at Hamburger Heaven to pick up dinner for everyone. I ordered my usual grilled cheese sandwich and French fries with hot sauce.

"Add a chocolate malt," Dad told the carhop. It was a special treat for me. All for less than a dollar. When we got home, I ran out to the backyard with a can of dog food for Blackie's dinner. I hurried back into the house to eat my dinner before it got cold. Not much of a meet-and-greet for Blackie. When Dad brings him into the laundry room for the night, I will tell him about my day and pet him. He likes that. I will tell him about the owners of the mansion where he was born.

I lay in bed waiting for Mom to kiss me goodnight. I thought about what a wonderful day I had because of the librarian. I learned that a stranger might help and inspire. I wanted to tell Mom about Elmira.

"Could my best friend, Janice, be a reincarnation of Elmira? They have a lot in common." I wanted Mom's wisdom.

"Comforting to think about. What was the librarian's name?" Mom wanted to know.

"I forgot to ask."

"Next time, ask," Mom replied, stroking my hair. "We are lucky to live in a place with an excellent public library. I went to school during the Depression. Everyone was poor. Many parents were immigrants and barely spoke English. I am sure schools had little money then. Students at my high school worked hard to succeed and graduate. Some went on to college. We wanted to be professionals when we grew up. I spent a lot of time at the library, too." I did not want to ruin a perfect day by asking her about my future as a writer. Maybe she was starting to see more potential in me.

Mom kissed me goodnight. I whispered, "I love living here. University City is a special place." I drifted off to sleep.

Chapter 14: Shortcut

Janice, Ashley, and I walked down Partridge Avenue to Heman Park after school. My Brownie troop organized a cookout where a murder took place. None of my Brownie troop members knew about the murder. It happened a long time ago.

Mrs. Townsend, Janice's mother, was the Brownie troop leader. While walking to the cookout, I wondered if there would be anything vegetarian for me to eat. I was starving. It was the last year to be a Brownie. The picnic celebrated our three years together. Being a Brownie saved me from being home alone one day a week. I would miss all the activities Mrs. Townsend arranged for us. I loved Mrs. Townsend. She got me. She taught me that a peanut butter and jelly sandwich tastes better made with toasted bread. She advised me to sleep on a towel in case I accidentally peed in bed, which happened sometimes. "Then you do not have to change the bed in the middle of the night." Great advice.

She gave me five dollars for cleaning her kitchen once because she knew I was saving money to buy a cockatiel. When we went to Velvet Freeze, she bought me double, sometimes triple, ice cream scoops to help me gain weight. Her daughters ordered one scoop. I was sure she would remember something vegetarian for me to eat.

I wished I had taken her advice about Blackie. She offered to take care of him. She knew Blackie needed more attention. "You can see him anytime, even when we are not home," she assured me. I could have slept over at her house. Then Blackie and I would sleep in the same room, just like I wanted. I should have been courageous and made the right choice for Blackie. Blackie would have had a better life, and I would not experience nightmares about him. I would miss Mrs. Townsend when I outgrew my friendship with Janice.

Janice, Ashley, and I were approaching the murder scene. There was a bridge to cross. Standing on the bridge, I gazed into the moving river, looking for turtles. On the other side of the bridge, the forest projected darkness. Walking past the scary, dark murder scene, I saw my Brownie troop at the old playground with swings, a merry-go-round, and teeter-totters. The playground had not changed since the murder. Creepiness coupled with a playground. I again turned my attention to the path between the trees and bushes. It invited me to the murder scene. I could be a detective when I grow up. Not really, I fainted at the sight of blood. I wanted to ask my friend Ashley to explore the scene with me. I shared scary stories and thoughts with Ashley, not Janice. Janice got upset when I talked about Nazis and that the Russians may bomb us. What did Janice think those school drills were about? I walked past the site without saying a word to Janice or Ashley. Here is the story Mom told me.

"Strangled with her garment while walking home from Heman Park swimming pool," Mom began her story of Ruth. "She fought her assailant. They found blood, skin, and the assailant's hair in her fingernails." Mom described the gory details.

The murder occurred eleven years before I was born. Yet, it was like yesterday for Mom. Ruth's brother, Sam, became the husband of Mom's best friend. "It was Sam who stayed up all night searching for his sister. Sam found Ruth's body at 6:30 the next morning. The police did little to help the family." I now understood the dangers of being in the woods alone. I thought of the woods around my mansion. I'll bring Blackie.

Then Mom came up with this, "Cities should not provide hiding places in wooded areas for criminals to hide. Criminals spy upon children while they play and then pick out their victims." I could feel a nightmare coming on tonight. I was so skinny someone might see me as weak and a victim. Plus, I played by myself. Easy prey.

Then the real kicker came. Mom continued, "Three boys were brought in for questioning. The boy with the last name of Williams was the suspected killer. Guess who one of the other boys was?" I shook my head, waiting for the big news. "Mr. Sabol. He was walking home from the swimming pool with the murderer. The murderer left the other two boys at the playground when he saw Ruth walk by and enter the path surrounded by trees and bushes. While the boys waited for Williams to return, he tried to kiss Ruth. He tried to do more. She resisted. He murdered her. He crushed her head with a rock." I did not understand, 'He tried to do more.' I did not ask.

Mom continued. "The newspaper said Mr. Sabol and his friend were sitting on the merry-go-round waiting for their friend, Williams, to return. Williams never returned. The two boys then walked to the path between the bushes and trees. Their friend was not there. On the path, the two boys found some of Ruth's possessions and took them home. They did not see her body pulled over to the bushes. When they heard about the murder, the two boys went to the police and turned in Ruth's possessions. They gave the police the name of their friend."

"What happened to the person who committed the murder?"

"He got off. Not enough evidence other than being a juvenile delinquent. He joined the army. Somebody killed him in the war. I am just glad he is no longer in our city. Once a murderer or rapist, always a murderer or rapist."

Mom must have made up the part about him dying in the war. I am sure the *St. Louis Post-Dispatch* did not run a heading about his death. If the paper published a list of the dead, his name was common, and it might not be the same person. I let her comment go. She was trying to scare me and not scare me. I wasn't sure I understood the word *rapist*. Too scared to ask what it meant. I am sure Mom did not realize she used a word I did not know.

Mom ended the story with this, "Never take shortcuts. Ruth was taking a shortcut home. She was hurrying home from swimming at Heman Park to help her mother cook dinner. Stay on the main streets where people are," she warned. Listening to the wisdom of Mom, I only took a shortcut once. It caused me stress and anxiety. Here is what happened.

A few years later, Ashley and another friend, Connie, became seventh-grade cheerleaders at Hanley Junior High School. Connie hosted a block party as a pep rally for the homecoming game. Almost everyone showed up. Ashley invited me to sleep over at her house after the party. Mom instructed me not to walk to Ashley's house in the dark. "If you need a ride, call."

When it was time to leave, all the girls wanted to walk to Ashley's house. I panicked and said, "My mom will drive everyone." They still wanted to walk. It was a warm, clear night.

None of them knew about Ruth's murder. I did not have time to explain.

They wanted to walk at night through the wooded grounds of the orphan home to Ashley's house as a shortcut. I heard the word, *shortcut*. Now I faced all the behaviors Mom warned against, such as walking at night without an adult when it was not Halloween, walking through a wooded area, and taking a shortcut.

In a panic, I asked Connie if I could spend the night. She replied, "Nancy is sleeping over." Maybe I should pretend I did not feel good and call Mom. Instead, I walked with a group of girls in the woods, carrying my overnight bag. The walk through the deep leaves and smells of fall calmed me. Ashley and I had spent many afternoons illegally exploring the acres around the orphan home. We walked by the Baby Jesus display. It usually scared me, but this time it was a comfort. I focused on the sweet lamb.

The next day Mom asked how I got to Ashley's house. I lied. The only lie I ever told. I made it. Ruth did not.

Chapter 15:
Becoming More of Me

At age twelve, I am focused. It may be a problem socially. Daydreaming absorbed me. Was I boring to others because I daydreamed when I should have been chatting? Was Louisa May Alcott a daydreamer? Did Louisa May Alcott have lots of friends? She had her sisters, which I do not.

My friend, Ashley, read adult political fiction books. She recommended books. I read them. I wouldn't say I enjoyed the books. "Stop reading children's classics. Move on," she advised. I was not sure I was ready to move on.

"Read *Animal Farm*, *1984*, and *Catcher in the Rye*." I was surprised Ashley promoted *Lord of the Flies* by Willian Golding. Didn't she see similarities between herself and Jack? Or maybe she was attracted to Jack? I preferred Ralph. Funny, I never recommended books to her.

Did Ashley read *Little Women*? I believed Ashley would find E. B. White's *Charlotte's Web* interesting. This book was a confirmation of my vegetarian lifestyle. I did not understand why more people did not become vegetarians after reading *Charlotte's Web*. Maybe they saw how skinny I was and decided it was not healthy. Ashley recommended a book I related to, Herman Wouk's *Marjorie Morningstar*. Marjorie daydreamed too. She aspired. I aspired. It was interesting to read what can damage aspirations. Boyfriends. Marriage gets in the way of fulfilling potential as well. I thought of Mom, who regretted getting married at age nineteen. Living with a mother who wished she was not a mother is challenging. Instead, Mom envisioned being a famous actress, renowned interior decorator, or prominent business owner. Did she want to be a lawyer? If she thought of marriage, it was to an intelligent, famous, and wealthy man.

One day I came home while Mom was cooking dinner and found her crying. Her nose dripped into the peas she was stirring on the stove. I got her a Kleenex. I did not ask her why she was crying. I have that image firmly planted in my memory. It was my responsibility to make her happy. It was an obsession and then a burden. I never succeeded.

I read *To Kill a Mockingbird* right after the film came out. I wished my name was Scout. My daughter could be Scout. I preferred reading books and then seeing movies based on the books. Many times, I learned of a book because a film came out. *Uncle Tom's Cabin* and *To Kill a Mockingbird* were the only books I read on prejudice against Blacks. Black was the new name Negroes gave themselves. Clarification, I did not read *Uncle Tom's Cabin*. Mrs. Townsend read it to me and her daughters, Janice and Judy.

I told Dad that Mrs. Townsend had read this book to me. Dad said, "Jews like this book. They translated it into Hebrew and Yiddish. They changed the plot in the Yiddish version. The Blacks are Jews. They are not enslaved. Instead, they are serfs. They become free by escaping to Canada."

Thinking about *To Kill a Mockingbird,* any person who was not White or Christian could have been the victim in the book. I believed an imaginary stone wall around University City protected me from the rest of the world. Almost everyone there knew I was Jewish. No one would say something horrific to me, such as, "They need to finish the job."

Dad told me it meant "Kill all the Jews." I heard this only outside the imagined stone wall. "Once you grow up, Linda Ann (he always called me Linda Ann) and are outside University City, you will hear all kinds of hateful remarks." He smiled, "Especially since you have blonde hair, light eyes, and a perfect nose." He leaned over and kissed me on the cheek. "No one will know you are Jewish."

"I want people to know I am Jewish. Jews need their own army in this country," I declared.

Dad lit his pipe, "Not a bad idea."

Reading helped me become me. There were lessons about life in each book. Books were companions. I realized I might not fit in with my old friends as I got older. Some were into mischief. Some were still into fantasy worlds. Some were athletes and signed up for soccer and swimming after school. I could not run fast. I feared the soccer ball. I swam wearing a nose plug I could not ditch. Mom was great. She took me to the YMCA, an old building downtown, for private swimming lessons. It did not help. Janice and Ashley decided to join a swim team. I wanted to join. I needed to be a stronger and faster swimmer. I could see divisions tied to talents and not friendship. I started a path of being more by myself.

The Jewish Community Center opened a new swimming pool out west. Hanging out with friends replaced lap swimming. Ashley's family joined, too. On weekends, our moms set up towels and chairs together. Both our moms wore Hollywood sunglasses and large-brimmed straw hats. Mom found Mrs. Sabol interesting. They chatted about politics, movies, books, and Mrs. Sabol confided in Mom about her personal life. They went to see Timothy Leary together. Mom came home all excited about LSD.

Ashley boosted my confidence by coaching me to jump off the high diving board. I loved it when I finally braved the jump. The fanciest jump I did was hugging a bent knee. I thought it looked more graceful. I was not going to dive off the board as Ashley did. She was always challenging me.

At Hanley Junior High School, where I would be going in the fall, I heard that being athletic was less important for girls. I wish I had known this earlier in grade school. Easier to wait it out.

Of course, Mom came to the rescue on this issue of picking teams for sports in grade school. I could hear her high heels hitting the tiled hallway floor as she walked to the principal's office. She called a meeting with the principal, Mr. Barnard, and the gym teacher, Mr. Deardorff. At the end of the meeting, team captains no longer chose teammates. We numbered off. Later, Mr. Deardorff revised the new rule. Each team captain could choose two players, and then we numbered off. That resulted in better competition between teams. I was proud Mom spoke up. It was humiliating for the same kids to stand alone after the athletes were chosen. I guess the other kids did not tell their parents about this ongoing humiliation, or their parents did not want to complain.

We anticipated the sex talk when the school year was just about over. Teachers termed it "Reproduction Education". Before showing the film, teachers threatened us with our lives. We could not laugh, talk, or engage in any behavior contrary to the seriousness of the topic, reproduction. We watched a film in class. We learned about sex hormones, the female menstrual cycle, fetal development, and sexual reproduction, along with showing diagrams of human anatomy. It seemed like some science fiction story. When I got home, I walked into my room, where we kept the *Funk and Wagnalls Encyclopedia* series. People who could not afford the expensive *Encyclopedia Britannica* bought these instead. Mom bought a new *Funk and Wagnalls* volume each week for $2.99 at the grocery store until we had the whole collection. I found them helpful. Sometimes, I picked a volume and started reading for random new information. Today, I was focused. I looked up reproduction in the encyclopedia. The book talked about some of the same information our teacher explained. There was a diagram of anatomy and an explanation of menstruation. The teacher said, "The penis goes into the vagina and sprays semen on the eggs, fertilizing them." I walked into the kitchen and asked Mom about it.

"Yes, that is correct."

"How does that happen? How does the penis get to the vagina?"

"The man lies on top of the woman and puts his penis into her vagina."

"Oh no! I am not getting naked. I'm going to wear underpants with a hole in it." Mom did not say anything more. Nor did I. Mom defended a teenager who lived off Partridge Avenue. This girl became pregnant in high school. Hearing Mom's sympathy for the girl, I knew if I got pregnant as a teenager, Mom would be kind and stick by me, not force me to marry. I was not sure what would happen next.

A few weeks later, we had our graduation ceremony. We were leaving a school that taught us we all had potential. We would turn that potential into career paths. Mom had a dress made for me. It was sleeveless, made of white eyelet, and trimmed in bright red. Red and white were the school's colors. We snapped a class picture. We danced. I danced with Ray Daniels for the last time.

Chapter 16:
Hanley Junior High School, A Transition

We received our class schedules. Looking it over, I realized the school administration made the mistake of signing me up for chorus instead of violin. The school office told me I must change all my classes to fit orchestra into my schedule. I liked the kids in my current section and decided to drop violin, a life mistake. The violin and Blackie were my bad decisions.

I have this recurring dream. I am walking the Hanley Junior High School halls searching for my math or French class. It varies. I have not been in school for some reason all year, and I am looking for these needed classes to graduate. A nightmare caused by quitting violin. Blackie caused separate nightmares. Every time the school orchestra played a concert, I sat in the audience wishing I was on stage playing my violin. Dad wished it too.

After walking home from Hanley one day, I knew I better take Blackie over to my mansion. The Adventist school moved away to their new location. I did not get to say goodbye to anyone. Dennis, a neighbor, told me that the mansion had a book sale, and he went over and bought several science books. I never received an announcement of this book sale.

I looked forward to Blackie and I having the mansion and the grounds all to ourselves. When we arrived, we found big signs that read, "No Trespassing". We entered the property anyway. Suddenly, the wind picked up, and all the large trees started swaying. I thought about the oak tree filled with honey that fell long ago. Blackie and I ran home. I told Mom we tried to go to my mansion one more time. "We came home because the trees were swaying."

She responded, "They were dancing their last dance."

Hanley Junior High School is a blur. What sticks out is the assassination of President Kennedy. We were in the school cafeteria, eating lunch and laughing about something. I chatted in my usual loud voice, a Dad trait. Our fun was interrupted by the loudspeaker, "President Kennedy has been shot. We will dismiss school." We were all confused and shocked. Our perfect place became scary. I did not know how to reach my parents. Luckily, Mrs. Townsend was waiting outside of school for us. She drove Janice, Ashley, and me home. Nobody talked on the way home.

When Mom, Dad, and Gary arrived home, Dad's initial comment was, "Thank God the assassin is not Jewish." My family repeated this after every crime. We did not want Jews blamed for anything. "It might cause retribution against all of us," Dad explained.

"Would people start killing Jews?"

Dad looked at me and responded, "People look for excuses to kill Jews."

After President Kennedy's assassination, I never stood by an uncovered window at night. I feared getting shot. I wondered if others had changed their behaviors, too.

I found junior high school socially challenging. I discovered cliques dominated. Walking the halls before school were girl cliques with corresponding boy cliques. The leaders of the cliques positioned themselves in the center, with their followers surrounding them. Think *West Side Story*. Riff and Bernardo were always in the center.

In one of these cliques, a few girls were stealing clothes made by Villager from Famous-Barr Department Store. They stored the stolen clothes in their school lockers and changed into these clothes once they arrived at school. I wondered how they washed them. I heard they went into the store's dressing room, put the expensive Villager clothes on, and then put their clothes over the Villager clothes. They casually walked out of the store.

Dad told me some department stores did not allow Blacks to try clothes on in the dressing rooms. If the clothes did not fit, the store did not let the Black women return the items. I thought these stores needed to monitor these rich White girls. I found these same girls to be mean to others. Do they wake up every morning before school and ask, "How can I be mean today?"

People were overly concerned with possessions, including me. Many boys and girls wore the shoe brand GH Bass Weejuns. We called them Weejuns. I researched the name. It came from Norwegian fishing shoes, wegian. They were penny loafers made in Maine. It was a shoe without laces that reminded me of the turquoise Indian moccasins Mom bought me. Instead of beads on top, these shoes had a strip of leather. Some kids slipped a coin on top of the shoe between the leather strips. They were sturdy leather, wine-colored with a rounded toe. Parents ordered these shoes through Boyd's Department Store. Sometimes, it took months to receive them. They were handmade. I would have to save up my allowance to buy these famous shoes if I wanted them.

I was a mess. My bra strap was too long and poked out of my collar. I finally cut the strap shorter. Non-important things became consequential. Bra size became a concern. Everyone wanted straight hair.

A ninth-grade boy approached me while I was standing in the school hallway. His hair was longer than most boys. He wore tan corduroy Levi's. Boys could wear jeans to school if they were corduroy. As a girl, I still could not wear corduroy pants to school. In protest, I wore culottes, pants that looked like a skirt. Back to this boy, his shirt was a Gant powder blue Oxford cloth. He wore brown suede desert boots. I admired his style. He said, "Don't worry. It's alright to be quirky. You'll figure it out." I smiled. Later, I looked up the word quirky in my pocket dictionary. I read *unusual in an attractive and interesting way.* Not bad, I said to myself. I never saw him again. I heard he moved to another school. Classmates transferred without saying goodbye.

I still felt embarrassed wearing my black and white saddle shoes, which I needed to support my flat feet. My saddle shoes were always untied. A friend quoted a poem to me called "Delight in Disorder" by Robert Herrick. "This line fits you, 'A careless shoestring, in whose tie I see a wild civility...'" I agreed. Yes, I was different. A theme was immerging. Sometimes I was a nonconformist or rebellious by choice, other times by my natural quirkiness.

One day while waiting in the hall for class to start, Bob walked up to me. "Let me show you how to keep your shoelaces tied." He did not appreciate delight in disorder. Or he thought I might trip on my shoelaces and fall. Mom always taught me to check my shoes before stepping on a department store escalator. He bent down and showed me how to tie a double-knot bow. From then on, I fastened all tie shoes with double-knot bows. Next, he became my hero when he showed up to school wearing black-and-white saddle shoes identical to mine. Popular Bob wore my dreaded style shoes.

Another hero was Alan. He wrote in my autograph book, "TO A SMALL PERSON WHO'S NOT BIG TO ANYONE EXCEPT IN PERSONALITY." Capital letters were his trademark. I reached for my pocket dictionary and looked up personality. I found this: *character or behavior particular to a specific person.* That fits. I liked the word, particular. I always remembered his kindness. Most kids signed stupid stuff. Luckily, no one called me Tiney Finey anymore.

Everything became complicated. I started to understand that a girl could drop a best girlfriend just as a boy dropped a girlfriend or a girl dropped a boyfriend. Do boys drop each other? Everything seemed temporary. One day I am happy and secure. The next day my new best friend drops me and is mean to me. Our car, Betsy, must have felt rejected when we traded her for the new deluxe Ford Falcon. I would have to find another best friend. I preferred just one best friend.

I met a permanent best friend, Sheila, in my math class. Mr. McFadden taught eighth-grade math. He caught me daydreaming. He invited me to the blackboard to solve algebra problems. Being in front of the class and standing at the blackboard stopped my daydreaming. I became more focused and ended up enjoying algebra. Working on each equation felt like solving a mystery. Mr. McFadden threw chalk at other students to get their attention. I heard Mr. McFadden threw an eraser at Gary Rich. Mr. McFadden helped those who struggled with math, and he helped those who were geniuses in math.

To help the geniuses, he contacted Washington University's Math Department. Mr. McFadden explained there were about 15 students each year that topped out of the math courses offered at the high school. Hearing this, Washington University stepped in and offered higher math classes for these students at no cost on the Washington University campus. University City had teachers who found opportunities for us.

Plus, Mr. McFadden rode his bike to work. I liked that. A boy told me to stop riding my bike. "Girls your age do not ride bikes." I was not about to give up my favorite activity for a boy. Pressure came from all directions.

After school, Sheila and I would do math homework at her house. When Sheila was sick and absent from school, I ate my lunch in a bathroom located in the basement of Hanley Junior High School. If I ate in the cafeteria, I had to navigate a hierarchy of the popular girls sitting in the middle and the less popular girls seated at the ends of the table. When it was nice out, I ate outside.

I decided to read and write more. Go to the library more. Hanley Junior High had an excellent library. I discovered I was wasting my time writing notes in class to classmates and then illegally passing the notes while teachers were trying to educate us. Trying to think of something to write was a distraction. I needed to pay attention to what the teacher was saying. I already suffered from inattention and daydreaming.

When I arrived home from school, I realized I better start on my homework. A report was due for Miss Fay's class. I remembered I had all those notes and newspaper articles about John C. Roberts in my desk drawer. I pulled out the yellow paper pad with all the newspaper copies hanging out the sides. I reread the articles and wrote about Roberts and my mansion. Here's the typed version.

> John C. Roberts December 17, 1853–April 27, 1924

John C. Roberts fought for principle, not personal gain. That was his legacy. Roberts' culture was Southern Democrat. He was prominent in St. Louis Presbyterian society. He helped sustain the Veiled Prophet Organization, centered around a mythical figure who was part of a secret society. Members owned the most prominent businesses and wealth in St. Louis. They were involved in civic and government leadership roles. They lived in mansions.

Roberts may have been the Veiled Prophet one year. His wife, Anna, and the wives of his good friends and business partners were all matrons of this organization. Its purpose was to raise charity funds. Anna was a member and officer for the Daughters of the Confederacy. Women back then were known by association with their husbands. Anna Roberts was only known in the newspapers as Mrs. John C. Roberts. She led an effort to erect a statue in Forest Park commemorating Confederate soldiers. That culture ran deep, filling a need to belong to a group. A newspaper picture showed a Southern belle party the Roberts hosted at their home, 1433 Partridge Avenue. Women wore traditional Southern belle dresses, and the men wore Confederate uniforms. Roberts' granddaughter served as a maid of honor in the

Veiled Prophet events. People all over St. Louis lined the streets to see the Veiled Prophet Parade. St. Louis became famous for this yearly activity.

John C. Roberts believed anyone who worked had opportunities. His personal history reflected this belief. He left home, Readyville, Tennessee, as a youth to seek employment. An opportunity came in Murfreesboro, Tennessee. There, Elzey Meacham hired and mentored young Roberts.

Roberts moved on from Meacham's general store business. Roberts preserved a deep gratitude to Meacham. Roberts held dear the fundamentals he learned from Meacham. He named his eldest son Elzey Meachem Roberts.

"I may not have another son," Roberts told family and friends at his son's birth. "It is more important to name my first-born son after the person who believed in me and taught me principles and skills, I continue to use than to name my son after myself."

Not only did Meacham mentor Roberts, but Meacham traveled to St. Louis in the 1890s to buy land in South St. Louis County. There he built homes for Blacks near a factory where they could work. Meacham offered housing and work.

In 1880, Roberts came to St. Louis as a salesman for Hamilton-Brown Shoe Company. Promoted to sales manager, he organized and entered the partnership of Roberts, Johnson, and Rand Shoe Company, which became the

International Shoe Company, one of the largest companies in the world. Roberts directed a branch of the International Shoe Company. He was a principal stockholder of the St. Louis Pump and Equipment Company, run by his younger son, John C. Roberts, Jr. In addition to all this, he owned the *St. Louis Star-Times* newspaper. It is puzzling the shoe company's manufacturing building became protected by the National Registrar of Public Places and the United States Department of the Interior. Yet, Roberts' home, a historic home, was demolished.

Roberts actively engaged in politics. President Woodrow Wilson was a friend. Wilson was quoted in the newspaper, as saying to Roberts, "since you know me." President Wilson traveled to St. Louis to campaign for the country to engage in World War I. The other time Wilson came to St. Louis was to promote joining the League of Nations. Roberts traveled to the White House to talk to Wilson about these issues. Both Roberts' sons served in World War I. Roberts met with St. Louis officials to organize a tribute to Wilson when Wilson died in February 1924.

Roberts was outspoken about Wilson's enemies, "Those with political and personal malice refused to support Wilson's efforts for world peace and goodwill. This was to be a Golden Rule for the world. Wilson's health broke under the stress and load of trying to bring world peace." Shortly after, Roberts died suddenly at his home in April 1924.

After I wrote this, I wondered whether Meacham's actions to build housing for Blacks inspired the Roberts family to do the same. Is that why the mansion was demolished and 22 houses were built for Blacks? Did the Seventh-Day Adventist Church and Roberts' family agree to do this? The Adventists used the mansion till their new school was built. I wondered, could the developer of this new subdivision have been an Adventist? The Adventists have an active movement to convert Blacks. I read this in the encyclopedia. Was this called "connecting the dots"?

A few days later, Miss Fay handed me back my paper. "I did not know all this local history you reported. Are you going to major in history when you attend college?" She assumed I was going to college.

"I want to be a writer."

"You could write nonfiction. It means you could look information up like what you did for this report and write books about what you find."

"I like your idea. How do I study to become a writer?"

"You could go to journalism school. You could study history and writing." I remembered the librarian talking to me about journalism.

"Our history books are boring. I am not sure I want to read them in college."

Miss Fay laughed. "Yes, they can be. That is why we do activities in this class. You could write books people want to read. Books concerning famous people. You could write a book about Mr. Roberts."

"I used to read the orange books in the library. They were biographies about famous people written for kids."

"You could write biographies about famous people for adults to read."

"Can you name me a few books?"

"Let me see what I have on my shelf. I have more at home. Here is *Profiles in Courage,* by President Kennedy." I walked over to her bookshelf. I saw a bird on the spine of a book and pulled it from the shelf. *John James Audubon,* by Margaret Ford Kieran.

She asked, "Do you appreciate birds?"

"I love birds."

"My mother gave that book to me when I was in grade school."

I was afraid to ask. I would not loan anyone my *Little Women.*

Reading my mind, Miss Fay replied, "Yes, you can borrow it."

"Thank you. I will take care of it." Miss Fay must like me since she trusted me with her copy of a cherished book.

"I know you will. Do you have a favorite author?"

"Louisa May Alcott." There was silence. That was the moment. "I could write about her."

"Yes, now you are onto something. Write about someone you feel strongly about."

I was overwhelmed with gratitude. Miss Fay opened more opportunities. I realized if my parents did not know how to direct my career path, Miss Fay could help me.

"The University of Missouri has a good journalism school. Go to the University City Library for a copy of the college catalog so you can read about the program. Do you go to the library much?"

I smiled. "The University City Library was my babysitter."

"Mine too." We both chuckled. "You could call admissions at the University of Missouri and ask them to send you a catalog. Call 411 for the number. Then you would have your own copy. There are journalism schools all over the country. If you have excellent grades, you might get a scholarship."

All over the country stuck in my mind. Finding someone who gets you is amazing. Miss Fay was that person. I was now on a course for the future. As I left her classroom, I read a new quote she posted on the bulletin board. *Sometimes it's the very people who no one imagines anything of who do the things that no one can imagine.* Alan Turing.

I arrived home from school and found my mansion gone.

Chapter 17:
1966 Diaspora

Dad worked in a city called Wellston. Erastus Wells created Wellston just as Edward Gardner Lewis created University City. Erastus Wells served in the United States House of Representatives in 1869 for eight years. He built the public transportation system in St. Louis. Erastus Wells was the father of the St. Louis mayor, Rolla Wells. Rolla Wells served as mayor during the 1904 World's Fair. The Roberts and Wells families were related by marriage, business, and politics. I report this history because I want everyone to know famous people lived in and visited the mansion. President Wilson may have been a guest, though I could not confirm. Newspapers only report some things.

At one time, Wellston was a prosperous area. It was about three miles from our home. As a little girl, I loved walking with my family along the main street, Easton Avenue. Easton Avenue was famous for mom-and-pop stores. Katz Drug Store was my favorite. They had everything, including a pet department. I questioned the morals of the store selling a monkey. I already established primates were like humans on my visit to the St. Louis Zoo.

Dad worked on Easton Avenue at the United Clothing and Furniture Store. Occasionally, Dad drove me to work with him. I spent the day exploring all the merchandise on display, watching TV, reading, and eating peanut bars from the candy machine. We drove in the surrounding streets, and Dad called on customers for their weekly or monthly payments to pay the balance of what they bought at the store. I stayed in the car.

Later, stores located in Wellston became burglarized, boarded up, or abandoned. I heard people say, "The neighborhood changed." Dad no longer took me to work with him. Dad was robbed a few times and pistol-whipped once. I will never forget coming home when Mom caught me at the door.

"Linda, Dad is resting. He is fine. Someone robbed Dad today. The robber pistol-whipped him. The robber took a gun and hit Dad in the face with it. His face is swollen, black, and blue. His one eye is puffed up. You can see him. He is OK," she repeated. "He is in pain."

I tiptoed into my parent's bedroom. Dad was sitting up watching the TV. I started crying.

"Oh my God," I exclaimed. I saw his eye swollen shut and his face discolored.

"I am OK."

"What happened?"

"I was leaving the store, walking into the parking lot. This guy was waiting for someone to leave the store so he could rob somebody. It happened to be me. Luckily, he only took my money, not my whole wallet. Ha, I did not have much, fifteen dollars. Luckily, I deposited money into the bank earlier."

"Did you resist at first, and then he hit you?"

"No, he had a gun. I gave him the money. Then he hit me to get away."

"Will the police get him?"

"No."

After this incident, Dad's employer hired a guard to patrol the parking lot. Crime got worse in the Wellston neighborhoods. Dad hired a bodyguard to escort him into Wellston neighborhoods when collecting money from customers paying off their purchases. The bodyguard, a customer's son, liked Dad and did not want to see Dad become a victim of violence. Dad said, "Robbers buy drugs. When there are few employment opportunities and poor education, people are trapped. Selling drugs becomes an occupation." The world confused me. I thought people robbed others for food and shelter. I needed to watch those new crime shows on television.

Here is how Dad's business worked. Dad drove to customers' residences to collect money they owed for merchandise bought at Dad's employer's store. At first, Dad had his own line of credit with the department store. He worked for himself. His customers bought merchandise, and Dad loaned them money at a high-interest rate. Some items had codes on them instead of a price tag. The salespeople would tell people the costs. The only way to collect the money was for customers to come into the store and pay on their accounts or for Dad to drive to their homes and collect money on accounts.

"It was difficult for women and Blacks to get credit cards. Husbands had to co-sign for their wives' credit cards," Dad told me. "Famous-Barr Department Store and other stores did not issue credit cards to Blacks. Some banks refused to issue checking accounts. That is why my business was popular with Blacks."

Around 1959, Dad sold a room full of furniture to a customer on credit. The customer did not make any payments. When Dad went to reclaim the furniture, he found it destroyed. Now Dad had to pay the store for the furniture. We were in debt for $5,000. That is a lot of furniture for a customer to purchase. I wanted to know if this included Dad's other obligations, credit he issued to other customers. I never asked. We did not have $5,000. It was a fortune back then. The store took away Dad's self-employment status. He had to work for the store and pay back the $5,000. The store owner deducted payments from his weekly salary. He paid what the customer owed him.

Dad would not have to pay back the debt if he declared bankruptcy. Mom refused. She wanted our credit and good name to be protected. I wondered if she regretted this decision. Some people did this regularly when their businesses failed. Later, she told me when we bought our new house in Creve Coeur, "We did not have any trouble getting a loan for the mortgage. We have a good credit history."

There were business owners in our neighborhood who declared bankruptcy and bought more expensive homes than the home we purchased. I thought about Mr. Frank. Maybe he did this too. Did he move to California because he declared bankruptcy? "It is not ethical," Mom said. "I do not care what others do." I looked up bankruptcy in an encyclopedia. Here is what I found.

Bankruptcy is a legal proceeding initiated when a person or business cannot repay outstanding debts or obligations. It offers a fresh start for people who can no longer afford to pay their bills. The bankruptcy process begins with a petition filed by the debtor, which is most common, or on behalf of creditors, which is less common. All the debtor's assets are measured and evaluated, and the assets used to repay a portion of the outstanding debt.

Mom always chose the high road. I wanted to know if her choice was the best in this situation. She said, "Others would pay for a mistake which Dad made and that was not right."

When Dad lost his business, our lifestyle changed. I did not care. What affected me was hearing my parents yell at each other. Mom lost respect for Dad.

Mom shopped for my clothes at the dime store. "Once you have good taste, you can find clothes anywhere," Mom explained. She cut off the sleeves of my shirts so they would become summer shirts. My parents rarely had a night out. Mom dreaded wedding invitations that required buying expensive gifts. Eagle Stamps helped pay for food at the grocery store. Mom sat at the kitchen table, deciding which monthly bills to pay. Dad talked about giving up his synagogue membership. Dad no longer bought a new car every three years.

All this connected me more to Louisa May Alcott. Her father also made unfortunate financial decisions forcing family members to work. It was not a problem for me. I always wanted to work. Having my own money was another path to independence. I continued to sell greeting cards. At least I was not selling junk from the kitchen drawer to the neighbors.

Mom became independent when she started a full-time job at the Missouri Division of Employment Security. Mom became a professional. She made it possible for people to secure employment. She told me this story.

"Many people applied. There was a line of people applying," Mom told me. "Somebody spotted me in the line dressed in high heels and my purple wool suit. This person called me out of the line. I was escorted directly to the interview. They hired me because I dressed professionally and had a great interview with Mrs. Weinrich."

Mrs. Weinrich became a cherished mentor to Mom. Mom never forgave Dad for his mistake. Yet, Mom became successful on her own because of it. I lived in a war zone between my parents. Whenever I took Dad's side, I got punished by Mom. Sometimes, I was mean to Dad in defense of Mom. Then I did not like myself. Life became topsy-turvy in all directions. I could no longer escape their bickering by running to my mansion with Blackie. Now, our very home may not be permanent.

When the mansion and grounds were destroyed, the 22 homes built in the mansion's place sold fast. By 1963 all these homes were occupied except for four. Buyers purchased the remaining houses at the builder's cost. Blacks bought all 22 homes. My family received numerous phone calls from real estate agents asking if the caller could list our home for sale. The answer was "No." Dad told the caller, "I am a real estate agent. I will sell my own home when the time comes."

The real estate industry targeted White homeowners to convince them to sell their homes using a scheme known as blockbusting. They created a panic that Black people moving in would lower property value. "Sell now because you are never going to get the money you want for your house," the caller declared, or the flyer read.

I started having more nightmares. I sleepwalked. Once, I was alone in the living room reading when someone knocked on the front door. I hid. Ashley, Janice, Mrs. Farb, and Mrs. Alper moved out west to Chesterfield or Creve Coeur. No one I knew was nearby if I had a problem at home. The neighbors I grew up with were gone. Gary worked at National Food Store after school and was rarely home. I could call Mrs. Daniels. I better add her telephone number to my list of contacts.

Dad called a neighborhood meeting. Dad hosted the neighbors in our rathskeller. I sat on the basement steps to listen.

"If none of us sells, our neighborhood will stay the same," Dad explained.

Another voice disagreed, "Well, the first three houses on both sides of Hazelwood have been sold to Blacks. Plus, Blacks now live at the end of our street."

Another man spoke up, "We were thinking of moving anyway."

A woman declared, "We looked at new subdivisions in Chesterfield. If we move there, the new house will have more space for the same mortgage payment."

A voice shouted, "For us, it's time to get a newer home."

Safety came up. "I do not want my kids walking home alone."

A mother asked, "Has anybody read the newspapers?"

Another mother responded, "Yes. Crime has increased, and the University City police department says they need to hire more police officers."

"The newspaper is accusing us of White flight," a man said.

Another added, "We are looking bad because people are moving." He continued, "Black people see our neighborhood as a safe place for their children to live with access to good schools."

"I keep thinking about what happened in Wellston when we lived there," an older woman lamented. "I did not feel safe going out at night."

"These new subdivisions out west have swimming pools and tennis courts."

"We no longer know who lives here and who is up to no good," another person claimed.

Listening to everyone's comments, I thought if my neighbors did not move, this could be an opportunity for two cultures to get to know each other. I wanted to stand up and tell everyone, but I lost courage. All this reminded me how the Presbyterians might have sounded, complaining about Jews moving into their neighborhoods, Lewis Park, and University Hills.

My neighbor who bought the Frank's house explained, "I am 70 years old. I downsized when I moved here. I do not want to move again. My wife is ill. I bought this home as my retirement home. I do not want to live in an apartment. I enjoy my house and its gardens." I felt terrible for him. After hearing him speak, I always said hi when we were both in our backyards. I continued cutting through his backyard when Blackie slipped through the fence.

Someone talked about a domino effect. Neighbors argued over the idea if they did not sell now, the value of their homes would go down. Homes were supposed to be investments. Dad explained, "The people moving in are hard-working." Dad and his committee lost the battle.

During dinner that evening, Dad explained, "Blacks receive credit to buy cars and merchandise at some retail stores. They can't get home improvement loans. If houses are not in good repair, then property values decline. I have a customer that only paints the front of his home. That is all he can afford. Another customer wanted to remodel a bathroom for his aging mother.

However, he could not get a home improvement loan. He works for Chrysler Motors and has a good-paying factory job. He earns more than me. He told me a friend he works with needs a new roof, and his friend can't get a loan for a new roof. Blacks may not receive loans for upkeep expenses if they move to our neighborhood. Most of these homes will need new roofs in the next ten years. Civil rights have a long way to go."

More neighbors sold their homes. A few classmates begged their parents to wait until they graduated from University City High School. After graduation, they would be off to college. While in college, it did not matter where their parents lived. Some parents did wait. Others moved out without saying goodbye. After moving, a few families arranged for their youngest child to temporarily and part-time live with a relative or friend south of Olive Street Road. These arrangements enabled children to graduate from their beloved University City High School.

My parents posted a For Sale sign after Gary graduated from University City High School in 1966. I would be fifteen years old when school started in the fall. "Linda may as well start a new high school in a new district," Dad told Mom. Our house sold in one day.

We found a display house for sale in Creve Coeur. I wanted it. Mom did not. "The dining room is too small," Mom complained.

"Look at all the closet space. Look at the bathrooms," I argued. "Each of us will have a bathroom. Well, Dad and Gary will share." I listened when Mom spoke with the developer about buying this new display house. I learned our new house payment would be less than the current one because we were getting another 30-year loan and had a sizeable down payment from selling our old house. Plus, the first month of living in the new house was free because the new house payments did not start right away. We felt optimistic about the move. Mom started thinking about reupholstering our old couches instead of buying new sofas.

"Those couches were expensive. They are comfortable and have many more years left." She continued, "I think cut blue velvet upholstery in the living room and the family room couch will have wide corduroy upholstery." She had me there. I love anything corduroy. I sensed she was enjoying the idea of a new house. I daydreamed about this new adventure. I would have a clean slate.

I loved the idea of buying a display home. It came carpeted, painted, light fixtures installed, trees and shrubs planted, and this house had a mirrored wall in the living room. It wasn't a used house. It was a new house without the wait for building a new place. Ashley's family lived in an apartment while the builder constructed her new home. I was glad we did not have to move twice.

Sheila helped me pack up at the old house and unpack at the new home. She was the organizer. Mom appreciated all her help. We stayed friends even though we went to different schools and lived about 10 miles apart. I discovered the St. Louis County Library about six miles from the new house. Plus, there was a Jewish deli, a pet shop that sold sunflower seeds for my cockatiel, and a small bookstore within walking distance from our new home. I had what I needed. Mom talked about getting me a job at the new Schnucks grocery store. "You can work in the bakery. You love bakeries." We started making plans.

The first morning in the new home, I said, "Mom, from the kitchen, I see horses." Mom and I started a new tradition of having morning tea together. "Let's plant flowers in the yard and under the picture windows. We can see them easily from the windows." Thinking of Wordsworth, I said, "I want to plant daffodils." Each room had a large picture window. The windows in our other house were high, and I had to stand on something to look outside. A glorious flowering crabapple tree was in front of my new bedroom window. I felt my room on the second floor was a tree house. "I'll have my tree again."

"What?" She did not understand I was thinking about our pear tree on Hazelwood Lane. I placed my cockatiel in front of the window with my red rocking chair beside my bird. I created a new place to read. Looking out the large window, all I saw was the crabapple tree. It gave me privacy.

I already had my eyes on a particular boy, John. He was a year older than me and not Jewish. I figured out a way to meet him. I stood right in front of him. How could he not notice me? Later, I found a book he once owned on the library book rack that contained donated paperback books. It was the *Odyssey* by Homer. I remembered seeing the title at the University City Library when I was ten. The story was about Odysseus trying to find his way home to his particular place and people. John wrote, "She's so Fine!" on the inside cover. It's a line from a favorite Temptations song. He circled the word, Fine. Now, I knew he liked me. Fine is the best last name, I told myself. I started singing "One Fine Day".

I took a school bus to and from the high school every day. It was a ten-mile bus ride through beautiful land, fields, and expensive homes, perfect for daydreaming. Parkway Central High School felt fake, not a real school. It was one story and spread out. I missed the feel of an Ivy League school that Hanley Junior High School and University City High School gave me. Parkway Central High School was a placeholder that launched me into the world.

At my new school, few knew I was Jewish with my blonde hair and strange-colored eyes. Didn't they know Fine was a Jewish name? I defended my religion and culture. It hurt the most when a new friend who did not know I was Jewish said something against Jews. Some classmates told antisemitic jokes. I started telling people I was Jewish up front. Let's get it over with, I thought to myself. I felt self-conscious about being a vegetarian but never about being Jewish. For the first time, I experienced being a minority. Being a vegetarian was just part of my quirkiness.

Reflecting on my old neighborhood, I learned a place supports different cultures over time. A farmer once owned the many acres off Partridge Avenue. The farmer sold the land to French Catholics, and they built mansions on these acres. Later, Presbyterians moved into these mansions and built more mansions on farmlands.

In 1953, Elzey Meacham Roberts sold the homestead where his family lived for 49 years. He moved to be near his contemporaries, his people. Adventists bought and used this property on Partridge Avenue as a temporary home and school. All this happened while Jewish people populated the surrounding area and most of University City. University City became a homeland for Jewish people.

Everything changed again in 1963 when the Adventists sold the property and moved. A developer razed the empty mansion and removed the trees, reflecting pond, arbor, and gardens to build 22 homes for another culture to become first time homeowners. Once again, everything ended, and everything began.

Moving away from my place, I learned I could live outside the shelter of University City when I was among people who accepted and understood me.

Epilogue

Thirteen years after we moved, University Forest Elementary School's population was 100 percent Black. There were 224 students enrolled. The school district wanted to close schools below 200 enrollments. About 350 students attended when I went there from 1956 to 1963.

University City discussed converting University Forest Elementary School into a magnet school in 1981. Some parents voiced concern about busing Black students to other schools in the district, south of Olive Street Road. These schools were predominately White.

Then it happened. The school board voted to close University Forest Elementary School by September 1983. Students were reassigned to Pershing School and Hawthorne School, still north of Olive Street Road. Current University City residents did not want higher taxes for schools. University City sold my elementary school and its property.

Over 20 years later, Ashley and I visited what was once our grade school. The building was the same, just converted to a nursing home. The playground resembled a ghost town. It looked just as we left it. The pullup bars and monkey bars remained. We still saw painted lines for softball, square ball, and dodgeball games. We experienced our pasts in this abandoned schoolyard.

Children, now adults, from the neighborhood had a "vague recollection" of the mansion. For me, it was a focus, a cherished memory, and an introduction to a love of nature. I felt free exploring the mansion's grounds. I met a different culture and felt at home. My intrigue with the mansion brought this culture and me together and gave me happy memories. A dog and her puppy connected us even after I could no longer legitimately visit my mansion.

A common St. Louis question is, "What high school did you attend?" The answer revealed ethnicity and economic status. Although I graduated from Parkway Central High School, I answered, "I grew up in University City." The answer translated to "I am Jewish." If I added north of Olive Street Road, I identified myself as middle class.

Each person I chatted with who went to University Forest Elementary School, Hanley Junior High School, or University City Senior High School in the 50s and 60s talked about receiving an education that could take them anywhere they wanted to go. My cohort became accountants, administrators and founders of non-profits, bankers, botanists, businesspeople, dentists, educators, electricians, engineers, entrepreneurs, lawyers, librarians, musicians, nurses, occupational therapists, physicians, scientists, and writers to name a few careers.

University City was our place. It offered children the freedom to explore a small city without fear. This freedom enriched our brains and helped us develop greater independence and creativity. I grew up navigating neighborhoods alone, which helped me feel capable and in control. While I walked home from a friend's house, I daydreamed I was walking across the country. I enjoyed being alone with my thoughts. My mind wandered to Louisa May Alcott. She daydreamed and wrote stories about her own life. Like her, I started writing stories in my head.

Particular Place and People

University City in the '50s and '60s embodied a place where a particular people built an ideal community as envisioned by the founder, Edward Gardner Lewis. Lewis was unaware his Utopia metamorphized into a Jewish Utopia. The community thrived grounded on family, education, being employed, and religion. John C. Roberts never knew his Crest Haven homestead at 1433 Partridge Avenue started equal opportunity housing in University City, Missouri.

Everyone I interviewed who lived on Hazelwood Lane or one of the surrounding streets during this time said, "It was like heaven."

Acknowledgments

My family, schoolmates, teachers, neighbors, and University City, Missouri, gave me a topic that became a passion. Many thanks to those I interviewed. Much gratitude to Isabella Roberts for her detailed memories of living at 1433 Partridge Avenue. I am deeply indebted to Gail Cleveland for reading and providing feedback on my first attempt at writing this book. She kept me going. Edward Levy provided guidance and editing. Deep love and appreciation go to my daughter, Erin, and husband, David. They encouraged me to keep telling this story. Erin created the book cover that captured my intrigue with the mansion.

I love my support birds. MoMo, my parrot, has been my screaming, chatty, and singing companion for over 50 years. Wedgewood, my cockatiel, brings me happiness with her excitement to see me.

I owe it all to Louisa May Alcott. Jo from *Little Women* inspired me to become independent and a writer.

Without a doubt, a pear tree connected me to history and helped me find my way.

Above is a 1900 drawing of the mansion before John C. Roberts bought the homestead in 1905 for $5,000. This is the picture I showed Bobby, John C. Roberts' granddaughter. The homestead is described as a double-stone home having 14 rooms with gardens of flowers and fruits. When I knew the mansion, it did not have a second-story balcony. On the left, a large bow window extended to the side lawn and provided a sunroom. I remember walking up the off-centered sidewalk to the steep porch steps and into the mansion.

Printed in the USA
CPSIA information can be obtained
at www.ICGtesting.com
LVHW051621041223
765671LV00041B/518